Mystery City

Mystery City

The Whitborough Novels

Alistair Lavers

Matador
9 Priory Business Park,
Wistow Road, Kibworth Beauchamp,
Leicestershire. LE8 0RX
Tel: 0116 279 2299
Email: books@troubador.co.uk
Web: www.troubador.co.uk/matador
Twitter: @matadorbooks

ISBN 978 1788035 507

British Library Cataloguing in Publication Data.
A catalogue record for this book is available from the British Library.

Printed and bound in the UK by TJ International, Padstow, Cornwall
Typeset in 11pt Aldine401 BT by Troubador Publishing Ltd, Leicester, UK

Matador is an imprint of Troubador Publishing Ltd

Dedicated to Bon Scott

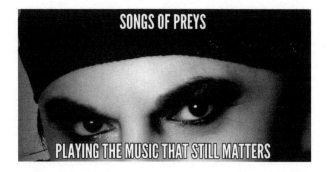

Contents

Precursor

The Yorkshire Coast, July 1645

Since the time when the first settlers began to study the constellations, within what is now the parish of Cayton, there has been an enclosure known as Caer Broc. It has long been in use, but offers little on first inspection within its borders to draw the interest of any traveller who may find themselves, for a moment, beside its boundary. The greatest length of it, adjoins a carelessly mended drystone wall of great age, which runs across the landscape in unequal courses. The wall's track follows the last ten miles of an ancient ley line, beginning at St Michael's Mount in Cornwall, through Glastonbury Tor and Avebury in Wiltshire, where it strikes out north from the cog of the great Herne's Barrow, through Tolbury mound in South Yorkshire and thence to the great bluestone circle on Landkey Island, two nautical miles north east of Whitborough. The wall's foundations were laid down long ago in prehistory by the people of the first age, and it still stands.

From the outlying fields of Cayton, where it first begins to rise and coalesce from the peat, in the flat valley of the Carr, the ancient structure slowly improves, until it reaches Whitborough-on-Sea's southern flank as solid and pleasing to the eye as any drystack wall in the county; finally terminating at Thumping Gate and the toll bar, behind the great earthwork ditch known as Sigurd's Dyke.

It is said, within the loose society of friends that still follow the first religion and the old traditions, that any man who disrespects the old wall's capstones, during Alban Eilir – the old Beltane festival of spring– should take care to bar his doors and shutters each night, until the next new moon, lest he be carried off into other realms, in the hours before dawn.

The last fellow to test the old legend did indeed vanish from his rest one night in April 1644, from a room at the Bell Inn, on Cayton High Street. What is not so well known, is the nature of the marks that were left behind – and what was found at the scene, after his disappearance.

The mysterious affair was the story of a single night – the first and last of his visit– when a powerful and vindictive gale blew up in the streets outside the inn, lifting tiles, rattling casements and stirring the trees around the vicinity. It was a curious occurrence, notable for the fact that the winds were most fiercely directed about the buildings close to the inn, and made such a bustle within the ivy that the landlord's dogs hid under the beds. Two witnesses, who later made sworn statements, attested that the landlord collapsed in a swoon the next morn after forcing the door of his strange guest at cock crow, investigating the cause of some terrible scream that was heard from within. He flatly refused to speak of what he had seen for days after – and was very much sick. Three other men also viewed the interior and were similarly afflicted in mind and body. The parson was called, ordered the room sealed and left the town before noon, never to return. No trace of Benjamin Comery was ever found, and the door to his room was never breached until the inn was demolished ten years later.

There are perhaps only two people still alive in the district who could give an account of the episode that matched the evidence. It was certainly shared within their families, but never to anyone outside the locality, though all written records and testimonies of the occurrence were freely available to the curious within the rooms of the town hall archive. The full facts may therefore have been more widely known than was readily admitted.

The incident would certainly account for the cold reception afforded to itinerant sellers of mistletoe and hawthorn, who were very badly received inside the town for some years after, all the offenders being followed or escorted in silence to the boundary dyke by the sheriff, though no explanation for their banishment was offered, or given.

From the seaward side of Caer Broc's boundary wall, the land descends before the blue grey depths of the Viking Ocean, eventually collapsing into jagged clefts where the heavy clay subsoil loses its grip on the soft bedrock beneath at the face of the cliffs. Too stony for cattle, though tolerable to sheep, it offers that particular kind of isolation that so improves the character of man.

Elias Rudkin, a shepherd of long standing and the present tenant of the field in the time of the last siege of Whitborough Castle, sat uneasily on the flat base of an upturned milking pail with his back to the sunset, surveying the windblown turf about his Dorsets. Alone with his thoughts and his irksome teeth, whilst his eldest boy Grundig slept fitfully on the small cot, within the close confines of their hut at his back. The monotony and the routines that went with the life of a shepherd, meant Elias did not care to record the names of the days between each Sabbath, only their number and passing, which he marked with a fresh notch on his crook at sundown.

Father and son – the shepherd and his apprentice – were two faces of an unbroken watch. One awake, one asleep, for the duration of the lambing, though the resting partner was still required to rise every third hour with a handful of coal for the small iron pot boiler stove, to keep the hotplate warm and their clothing dry.

In the warmer months, the small ventilation hatch cover in the last course of boards, below the roof shingles, could be removed completely, though during the last few nights it had been set down for a different reason. Elias had spent a restless night under the spell of a strange dream which seemed connected to the coming storm and troubled his waking hours.

The two men had been waiting expectantly for days, listening for the sound of a pistol report; not the sound of the gun of a stranger, or a Cayton huntsman in the weald, but the sound of a gun belonging to them alone, which now covered a switchback in the path through Elvenhome ravine nearby. Cocked and bound to a hazel frame, staked to the ground and concealed under oilcloth, to protect it from rain, it was topped off with a dirt-encrusted fleece, speckled with urine and weighted down with rocks. A bow cord, tied tautly to a tree on the opposite bank, cut across the footpath at knee height, curled around a branch smeared with goose fat and disappeared through a small tear in the tent to the trigger, through a ring bolt hammered into a tree root. The fleece was added as a precaution, to weight down the oilcloth against the wind, and keep foxes, badgers and boars from knocking the mechanism.

The pistol, a patilla-style miquelet flintlock, had come into the possession of the shepherd by fate and providence. Washed ashore on the storm tides the previous winter in an olive wood case, within a larger chest, protected against moisture and water ingress by a gasket of catgut and honey tar, it was a rare and desirable firearm. But to Elias, its primary value lay in it being unknown and untraceable to him. It would be – he hoped – a tool for his enrichment and the beginning of a new life, the comforts and riches of which he could still barely start to comprehend.

These intentions had taken form quite by chance –by the simple accident of overhearing the details of a plot hatched by four local adventurers on his boundary one night, to steal a strongbox of gold and jewels which the besieged garrison at Whitborough Castle were desperate to spirit away before the garrison fell. Elias and his son had no history or experience of criminality, outside of poaching. Despite this, they had decided to take what they thought might be a fair risk for the chance of acquiring riches beyond their dreams. They already possessed an advantage over the men who would come through their territory – they had a better knowledge of the terrain through which gold would come than any man guarding it, and the wit to exploit it.

The last winter of 1644 had been long and cold; snow

fell late in January 1645. The British Isles in this period was in the grip of what historians and climatologists would later refer to as the Little Ice Age. Many slow-flowing rivers froze to depths safe enough for horses and wagons to traverse their widths. In the years after the civil war, London held ice fairs on the River Thames, and the ground froze in Somersetshire to depths of four feet. Agricultural communities were hit hard, as the cold thinned out the weak and sickly amongst their livestock and their masters. Magistrates began to meet more and more men of farming stock inside their courts, as families resorted to desperate measures to pay their creditors. Suicides reached crisis proportions and death stalked the highways and byways of the provinces in the guise of brigands and highwaymen. Coal became so precious a commodity that Parliament ordered an army to Whitborough to end the attacks on the coal barges that were so essential to the comfort and warmth of the populace of London.

Elias had also suffered. The extreme weather had caused him the loss of many animals, though the Dorset Horn and Poll Sheep of his flock were able to lamb all year round and would soon recover their numbers in the spring. Not reliant on a high level of nutrition, they produced abundant wool and a good carcass. In the meantime, he did not go hungry. On the same night, after the priming of their pistol trap, in the last minutes before sundown, a rapping sound was heard on their steps. Father and son were in the midst of exchanging places inside their hut, tossing lice from the seams of their sheepskins onto the coals in the stove.

'Good greetings inside. Wilt thou answer to a servant of the Lord?'announced a familiar voice, which they reasoned was connected to the knocking a few moments earlier.

'Tis the parson father,' whispered Grundig nervously, 'we muste answer, muste we not? But why is he come? Not for mutton, for silver?'

'Why indeed boy – itt is not for these things I'll warrant. The houre of his visit speakes of some other intent – I am not reassured,'muttered Elias as the gusting winds outside whistled through the reed-thin gaps between the joints in their roof.

'Speake low father…'

'Be att ease lad, we cannot be heard without, when the windes make such play in the roof. Dost thou hear other voices now boy? Thou muste be my ears.'

'No, none other father.'

'Then we should meet oure pilgrim. If he cometh alone.'

'Elias! Wilst thou come now to parley? I am att thy door!'called the parson once again, in a cordial but insistent manner.

'Proffer him the stale milk, in the slops jugg. Twill curdle his passion for oure company,' smiled Elias, impishly. 'I am inbetween pantaloons parson! Grant me time to arrange myself,' shouted Elias, for the benefit of his unwelcome visitor outside.

'Ay father, this morsel will heap more discomfort on its sourness,' added Grundig, snatching up a small damp folded parcel of sacking, into which they had wrapped a piece of cheese which was beginning to fester.

'Be swift Grundig, into the milk then and let us be cunning – like our Lamb of God.We shall tell oure guest that ye are struck by a pox of the throat boy, speake not and cough generously.If he does not curtail his visit then, we shall both have cause to guard oure tongues.'

As the living cheese was decanted into the milk, and living it most certainly was in the purest sense of the word, one of his dogs began to bark from the bottom field. It was not a territorial kind of bark or a warning, but the fast, repetitive howling of an animal maddened by fear. Elias, sensing danger, lunged for the door, knocking the bolt from its collar as he pushed on its planks. Then as quickly as it began, the noise suddenly ceased, following a brief squeal and a whimper. All three men, Elias, Grundig and their visitor, the parson, were now outside looking downwind in the twilight, distracted from their imminent business by the sudden interruption. Their other dog Jasper had run up the incline from its lean-to den lower down and was now under the hut, quivering beneath the rear axle rod, mewing like an injured puppy. Grundig observed the flock was running up the pasture as one mass towards the shelter of a hawthorn-ringed copse at the very edge of the upper field.

'Father…,' cried Grundig, 'look to the flock! The Devil's beasts are come agayne!'

'Boy, string thy bow and bring oure last pistol!'growled Elias.'AND THOU!' he bellowed, seizing their speechless guest by the shoulders,'can stand wyth us and send them to hell with thy booke of spells!'

'NO, ELIAS… I CANNOT! I have no power o'er them. I…'

'Ye have the most powerful book in all the worlde parson, and divine protection. We have no such armour, but will gladly do battle with these fiends because we have no hiding place left us in the worlde.'

'Elias, there is naught to be done here, we muste shelter or be ripped apart,' wailed their visitor beseechingly, all his pompous arrogance gone as he joined the sheepdog in its panic, trying to push his way into the hut.

'I would rather that than die of hunger – a pauper. I go to my fate. Stand aside.'

Downwind from their hut, a fast-moving, indistinct mass began to emerge from the darkness in the lower field. Growing in size and detail, it ran towards the three men from the last place of the howling dog. It was as dreadful a thing as any of them had ever seen, in life or described in scripture, as swift and rough-haired as a wolfhound, but as thick and muscular as a bear from the dark northern forests of Saxony. Elias, acting quickly, hefted the silver-tipped lance of cedar, handed down to him from his father; weighting the belly of the stave in his palm, as he felt for the midpoint – the fulcrum– and drew back his arm.

'Aim true now lad. Hold firm and aim true… NOW!' shouted Elias to his offspring, as they fought to keep their courage from deserting them. His son's pistol cracked and the ball struck the black form sprinting towards their feet, slowing its run sufficiently for Elias to judge his throw. Then the lance flew with all the power in his arm and shoulders into the mass of the creature which the pistol shot had temporarily checked, ending its charge; the beast folded in upon itself and slumped hard onto the turf, writhing and howling, shedding great handfuls of fur.

'STAND NOW– COWARD!'shouted Elias, scolding the diminishing figure of the parson who was fleeing the field, scampering and stumbling blindly after the flock.'

'Father!'

'Oure protector has beshitt himself!' yelled the shepherd, mocking the stumbling preacher who was scampering away as fast as his short legs would carry him. 'Leave him now, protect me boy! I go for the lance. Barbed broadheads on your string!'ordered Elias, instructing his son.

Elias ran to the place where their first attacker was dying, pulling the spear from the black hide of the monstrous cadaver which seemed to be collapsing in upon itself.

An arrow whipped past his shoulder as he knelt down and he raised the tip of the spear again, jamming the blunt end cap into the stony ground, to stiffen the shaft against the second Hell-hound that would soon hurl itself upon it. Then the feathers of the arrow which had passed him so closely came back into view, shaking like a trembling hand as the thing into which they were fixed sprinted toward him. Another arrow, from Grundig's bow, slipped passed his arm then the second creature flew at the tip of his lance, its mouth red and bloody, howling with hate. Elias braced the lance with all his strength, whispered a prayer and shut his eyes.

Chapter One

Jungle Rock

'Damien, who were those two men in the black overalls?'asked Mitsu Yamada, one of the four waking night security staff at Charlwood Zoo, as she approached the gate to the rhino enclosure with her partner. 'Were there any maintenance appointments for tonight, I did not see any contractors passes left out for us?'

'Them two in the masks?'

'Yes. I am sure I have seen them before somewhere, did you recognise them also?'

'Nope –never seen'em before.'

'It was the way one of them was walking. I have seen someone here before walking strangely like that.'

'Let's just see what's spooked Edith first. Do you see any foxes or badgers about?'asked Damien, as he stepped up to the padlocked metal bolt on the gate. 'Your eyes are better than mine.'

'I cannot see anything now. Would you like the torch?'

'No. Just leave it off for the moment Mit, it'll only wind her up even more. She must have stopped charging about inside, she's just snorting and breathing heavily,' said Damien hesitating, holding the fingers of his free hand against his earpiece. Let's do a circuit and check the outside first,' he said, putting away his keys. 'She's probably just woken 'erself up farting. Check your safety's on too,' he added warily, pointing to Mitsu's rifle, 'we don't want any more accidents this year, or the guvnor might lose his licence and we'll be out on our arses.'

'*Out on our arses?* Is similar to something I already hear…'

'It's Yorkshire slang for losing yer job.'

'Oh. It is rude? I have also heard a close expression "out on your ear". Arse is bum– yes?'

'Aye, "out on yer ear" is for the company of yer elders an' betters; and "out on yer arse" is just amongst friends.'

'People say my language – Japanese, difficult to learn. I think English!'

'Well lass, there's a few friends o' mine would agree wi'ya there. They can't speak proper English either.'

'Do you smell that?' Mitsu asked, wrinkling her nose suddenly.

'What – the dung?'

'No. That *chem – ical* smell– how you say? It smells like air freshener – or ozone. Can you smell also?'

'Now you mention it, I did catch a bit of a whiff of something. Smells like that gloopy lemon disinfectant stuff the cleaners use in the bogs.'

'Why would that smell be here?'

'Mebee them two blokes have been using it in t'sewer pipe junction.'

'Oh.'

'There's an inspection hatch cover at the back of 'er shed. It links up wi' t'mains sewerage pipe that runs by front gate. We probably just caught the smell o' somethin' coming out o' that.'

'Ah, so you are right – how are Edith's breathings now?'

'Her arse is breathing fine.'

Dave and Brian Drake, the men responsible for Edith the Rhino's intemperate outburst, were striding briskly away from the scene of their aborted visit to her stable block, still without their property –a red Snap-on toolbox full of gold doubloons that their nephew had hidden behind her storage bins in a fit of pique.

To reduce the risk of vomiting from the smell of the young rhino's anal emissions while they were creeping about inside her bedchamber, Brian had foolishly added a small glug of car air freshener concentrate into the filter cavity of his decorator's mask, though its effect on his vision and sense of balance had been far from neutral.

'Ocean breeze… more like kamikaze wind…' groaned Brian, trying hard to ignore the throbbing headache that the air freshener fluid had induced. 'Smells like bloody screenwash. I'm gonna kill that stupid little bastard; sticking my gear in a bloody rhino enclosure – is he off his friggin' head?'

'Do you want to try again in a while Brian, when it's calmed down again?' asked Dave, his brother.

'Tonight? No way – the bloody thing'll be wired for the rest of the night now. What the hell did you tread on? Oh God – I think I'm going to throw up…'

'I stood on one of its bloody footballs.'

'Didn't you see it?'

'Of course I didn't bloody see it. If I'd seen it I wouldn't have bloody stepped on it. It was under the straw. Are you all right?'

'I feel a bit queasy, it's that stuff I put in the mask… all this for a fistful of coins.'

'You managed to get some!'

'Just a fistful. I'd got one hand in the top drawer. I just hope I put back enough hay to cover the floor in front of its storage bins before we had to leg it.'

'Is it locked?'

'Oh yeah. At great personal risk I might add. I'm not going back in there, with great grunting Bertha again. We'll have to find some way of getting it out of its shed with some kind of bait, so we can go back in and get our stuff, without being mauled, flattened or punctured. Keep your eyes open a minute,' said Brian, disappearing quickly behind a conifer to retch.

'What are you doing Bri?'

'Bringing up me tea, if you've *got* to know.'

'The feeding hatch is jammed Damien,' whispered Mitsu, noting the buckled wooden shutter on the side of the stable. 'She must have struck the frame with her horn.'

'Okay. We'll log it when we get back inside an' maintenance can fix it tomorrow. There's nowt else out o' place that I can see. Let's get back and put t'radio on – see if there's any more news abaht that ship exploding.'

'Damien?'

'Mmmm?'

'There's something shiny on ground there, next to her scratching post. It looks like coin.'

'Pick it up and bring it wi' you. You never know, it might be lucky.'

4

Dave and Brian ducked behind a huge stone statue of Pan, on the edge of the drive, as the other pair of night security guards drove past in their van; pulling up at the bottom of the steps in front of the house to speak to Lord William Henry who was on his way to the rhino enclosure.

'What the hell's that daft old bastard wearing now?'

'Who?'

'Him – Lord Whatsisface…'

'Woollens?'

'Lord Crackpot.'

'Look at that thing he's holding. It looks like a ruddy rocket launcher made from a vacuum cleaner.'

'Let's get back to the Saab, one near-death experience is more than enough for tonight.'

Chapter Two

Saturday Morning

Charlwood House, the ancestral seat of the Warner Woollens family, lay within an arrow's flight of the Cloughton to Whitby road. Four miles distant from Cloughton village and six miles south from Robin Hood's Bay, it appears abruptly to the unready eye of passing motorists on the A171, at the top of a low ridge, between two dark blocks of forest.

Built in the Palladian style, in Bath stone, around a central three-storey building crowned by a large triangular pediment over Ionic columns, it had two large wings, set back slightly from the main building and identical in style to the central edifice. The ridge of the main house roof ran east to west and was slated. Each wing featured a conservatory-style roof at right angles to the main house, set within a lead gulley and surrounded by a rooftop walkway ringed by a waist-high stone balustrade. Two sets of steps directly in front of the main portico – and also at right angles to the house – connected the lower gardens to the terrace, which ran the full length of the front of the house.

The surrounding estate ran to nearly two thousand acres of coarse woodland, undulating fields and wild moorland between the River Esk and the A171, the main road from Whitborough to Whitby. Before the establishment of the zoo, the estate drew its income from logging and hosting shooting and walking parties, the woodland supporting a large breeding herd of deer and wild boar. There were also many firm alluvial banks, stream pools and jetties on the western banks of the Esk, from which the estate's guests could fish on the river and its tributaries.

The present Lord Woollens– William Henry– had built a considerable fortune in his own right through investments in several large construction companies at the start of the motorway construction boom. This allowed him to indulge his passion for exotic animals and reptiles. Unlike many zoos, Charlwood maintained an indoor reptile house in a south-facing corner of the estate, attached to an annexe of the boiler house, where visitors could study the large collection of snakes and lizards. There was even a breeding pair of Komodo dragons, Stan and Hilda, in their own, purpose-built enclosure. Underfloor heating, insulated earth bank walls and thermoplastic roof panels ensured the 'desert house' kept its exotic tenants at a comfortable 28 degrees Celsius, whatever the temperature outside.

The main bathroom in the family wing of Charlwood House was almost as large as the footprint of a typical Victorian inner terrace. In winter, the first Lord Woollens could sometimes be heard rolling boules along the tiled floor of his water closet whilst *enthroned in spirit*, awaiting the arrival of spring. Lord William Henry was inside enjoying a shower and a sing-song of the kind only a sufferer of aphasia, or a member of the Bonzo Dog Doo-Dah Band could better.

'You be– my rexy dinnerlady – I'll be your king,

You be – my ma – mamar malady,

7

My chips are gin…'

His song, such as it was, was suddenly interrupted by a call from his butler on the voicepipe. 'My Lord, Ibrahim wishes to speak to you when you have showered and dressed. He's awaiting you in the library.'

'I'll be quickettycan Haskins.Betsyheavenses! It's been a night of f-fun.'

Ten minutes later, Lord Warner Woollens returned to the gloriously gilded, decadent splendour of the master bedroom, dressed in one of his favourite Sandhill Tweed three-piece suits, brushing out his hair and beard. He approached one of his closets and opened the doors, stepped inside and unclipped the sling of his great ancestor's repeating crossbow from its hanging rod and fastened it around his shoulder, balancing the great weapon on his chest, before retracing his steps, looking like some corrupted Daliesque vision of a medieval crossbowman.

When he had first been disturbed, just before midnight hours earlier, alerted by the home-made status alarms dashboard beside his bed, he had taken out his spear gun but thought better of it after accidentally discharging it into the floor above the staircase. Now, six hours later he was up again, though his wife, Lady Antonia, was far from pleased at being disturbed in the midst of her reverie; but not so uninterested in her husband's labours, that she was going to withhold her waspish observations.'William… where are you going with *that thing*?'she snorted,observing her awkwardly retreating husband through a narrow gap in her damask and cashmere eye mask.

'The alarm board began to blink again this morn Antonia, though it was an amber light, so there is no need for me to be there straight away. But I am pervyclothed and clothyprepped now,' he replied, turning himself about, to address the small hill under the bedspread which had come back to life.

'Then why do we employ all these people, twenty-four hours a day if not to ensure you get a decent night's sleep?'replied the mound.

'The staff still need my advice and guidance from time to time my dear and the benefit of my executive eye, especially when one of our most precious new beasts is out of sorts.'

'You're certainly not going to help matters turning up with one of your grandfather's unholy contraptions; it'll put the fear of God into that poor bloody Japanese girl... Whatever *help* you can offer is going to be somewhat diminished if it goes off in company. It should be in a display case in a military museum, where it can't do any more harm.'

'The Warner Woollens cartertridge machine crossbow is one of my ancestors' greatest achievements, Antonia; and as good and safe as any Winchester or Martini-Henry, if handled respectfully. Now I must go and speak to Ibby. He's been waiting patiently for me in the library.'

'Just don't leave it where someone else might pick it up. Remember what happened to Incapability (the estate's head gardener). We were jolly lucky he didn't sue, and now we're the only family in the district that actually subsidises our groundsman's bar bill to help him forget about the pain of being speared by *that thing*.'

Chapter Three

Up Around the Bend

The same morning in Cloughton village, several miles north of Whitborough and two miles from the estate, a Caledonian Ptarmigan tour coach, with a works party from Fort William, drew up in front of the Shirestones Hotel and began to disgorge its passengers onto the single skinny pavement opposite, blocking out the light and most of the road for the six small cottages directly behind the bus stop and shelter. The young and old, couples and children, carried their cases and belongings between the cottage fronts and the side of the luggage bins. They then started to emerge either side of the coach's bodywork, peering out nervously onto the high street from the offside taillights and front grille to check the road was clear before they dashed across the narrow strip of tarmac onto the hotel's forecourt which was crammed with small round table and chair sets, squeezed together beneath their accompanying branded sun umbrellas.

Daisy Mae, Robert Cunncliffe's eight-year-old Yorkshire Terrier and the last occupant of the coach, began to whimper and tremble again as she was carried yelping from their seats for the second time in her tartan travel caddy. Mr Cunncliffe had set down her little stoneware drinking bowl and a small dish of bacon scraps on the kerb a few minutes previously.

His poor pet had leapt back into the coach and was cowering under a seat near the middle aisle, refusing his generous offer of crispy chicken skin and mayonnaise left over from his lunch. Since the coach had parked, Daisy Mae had already nipped his ankle and relieved herself on the breast of his polo shirt before they were even disembarked; all because his dog had caught the invisible scent pheromone trail of their host, who was having a few difficulties of his own. Not with his arrangements, or his guests, but with his new alter ego: a vicious, moonstruck, twenty-five stone carnivore with five inch fangs and constipation.

Lindsay Boldwood – the landlord of the Shirestones– and the source of Daisy Mae's inexplicable angst, had assembled his usual complement of extra staff, drawn from the sons and daughters of the village for the Easter break. He was checking every detail before the arrival of his guests; unwittingly impregnating the air inside and outside the premises with a scent that was guaranteed to send every cat, dog and corvid in the immediate vicinity into a paralysing fit.

Dale and Matthew Penny, the twin sons of the local vicar, home from their first spring term at Cheltenham Art College, worked between the bars and restaurant.

Gemma and Bonnie Westmorland, his regular part-time staff, the daughters of John and Carol Westmorland of Wythall Farm, were also on duty for the Bank Holiday weekend to clean the bedrooms, ensuites and toilets, see to the laundry, lay the tables, and cut and arrange fresh flowers in the corridors and lounges. They were about to experience the most extreme set of circumstances of anyone at work in hospitality and the pub trade since the Second World War. By Tuesday morning, Dale would be bald, Matthew would have

11

developed a permanent nervous hiccup and the girls would have moved as far away from the countryside as possible and would probably never pick up a copy of *Little Red Riding Hood* again.

Boldwood had recently become a live carrier of an ancient Nordic strain of a lychanthropy virus that had nearly cost him his livelihood the previous Tuesday, the occasion of his first transformation. Whitborough was now one video store proprietor short, as a direct consequence of his wolfish urges. He had also devoured, in reverse order – a much loved Gloucester Saddleback boar and two house cats, one of which had been close to his heart, but had died a few inches away from the very same organ on its journey down his oesophagus.

The ancient, mutated lycanthropic virus – which had erupted in the flesh of their employer a few nights before – had once been widespread in Scandinavia, but had almost died out before its arrival in the British Isles. Around three to five per cent of Scandinavians still carried a dormant version of the condition, but of those, only a tiny percentage would go on to suffer full-blown attacks. For this to happen, the infected subject must have been born when Mars was in transit through the sign of Aries, in the twelfth house of the subject's birth chart. In astrology, Mars is said to be exalted or *in dignity* in Aries, whilst the twelfth house, in astrological tradition, is the place which governs the hidden self, the unconscious. The house of secrets.

As well as the northern European strain, there were also Balkan and Indian forms of the disease, which also required the same astrological conjunctions, but this branch of the virus had never spread out into the other races as effectively as it had done within families who were of Nordic descent.

Once the sympathetic host is fully mature, the virus goes active in the hypothalamus, at the next full moon, or the first full moon after the completion of puberty in the young. Only when the first full transformation has been achieved is the victim able to change whatever the position of the moon, during times of great emotional stress or anger, but still only during the hours of darkness. Strong ultraviolet light on twenty percent or more of the incubator's exposed skin area or foods with a reasonably significant magnesium content will inhibit the ability of the virus to produce sufficient quantities of lychanthropic hormone to effect a full change. Instead, the subject will develop and shed up to two coats of body hair during their deepest sleep cycle. This postponement will also increase the life expectancy of the subject, to a greater or lesser degree, if the transformation is continually frustrated. Some retain the memory of their time as the wolf, others hold no memory whatsoever. Lindsay was one of the latter, but would soon become one of the former.

What Boldwood could not know was how brief his life expectancy now was, if the transformations were not arrested. His heart muscle would rupture and fail catastrophically within the span of five years, unless a ruptured spleen or an intracranial haemorrhage struck him down first.

Such is the power of the change, it completely transforms the skeleton and soft tissues in under a minute. In reverse, the process is much slower to return the animal to its human form – taking up to ten minutes –while the emerging human suffers severe neurological pain and nausea, sometimes lasting several hours. The physiology of carriers also dictates their form as the wolf, producing either pure or mixed mesomorphic, ectomorphic or endomorphic forms. Constipation in the host will also affect the final size of the animal, often increasing its size by up to a third. Boldwood was the largest werewolf in the history of mankind.

Inside Clash City Records, on the edge of Whitborough town centre, Brian Drake had just agreed to gulp down another mug of black coffee from Corfe's Café, to take his mind off the pickle he was in. With a fortune in stolen gold at the zoo, fifty courses of anabolic steroids and Dianabol, under the dog's bed behind the counter, and the possibility of fifty impatient doormen beating a path to his shop on the busiest day of the year, he was feeling distinctly uneasy. These problems would have been more than enough for one caffeine addict to cope with, but Brian was also the brains behind the biggest multiple terrorist attack in mainland Britain and had just been informed by his one-legged South African shop assistant that he didn't have enough Twisted Sister t-shirts to last the weekend.

'Michael? Go an' get us a toasted teacake from that mad Irish bitch down the passage will you. Make sure she doesn't put half a tub of Lurpak on it. I need to live at least until the end of the week. When I've scoffed I'm gonna nip out to the library.'

'The library? But it's full of books Brian.'

'Well I hope they've got one about rhinos, or I'll have to nick one from Smith's.'

Chapter Four

The Carr Wold Parkway Incident

It was late on Saturday afternoon when the media descended on Whitborough in force. The terrible events of Good Friday had occurred too late in the day to make the Saturday papers, but the editors of the nationals were determined to run an in-depth post mortem of the Bank Holiday mayhem, with the full involvement of all their departments in their Sunday editions and despatched their reporters to scour the town for witnesses, instructing them to find themselves a room in a hotel, or bed and breakfast. By Saturday teatime there was no accommodation left in the whole of the borough and desperate hacks were driving to Filey and Whitby or into the villages of Hunmanby, Cayton and Aveyou Nympton, in an attempt to find a room for the night.

Every television channel and radio show was running their own story of the sinking of HMS *Brazen* and the terrorist attacks at Carr Wold Parkway and Wyndell Bank railway tunnel, as well as the events before and after the attacks, including the bomb scare and the amateur film of a brawl between the Navy and the Milk Race Cycle team, which the news team production staff at *Look North* had been salivating over. Both the BBC and ITV had decided to present the events in a way which was going to be very unflattering to the authorities and the government. The ministers and civil servants who could be found were recalled to Whitehall, and Parliament held a bad-tempered emergency session, in which many new faces from the back offices of state were thrust into the limelight, to take the place of their superiors who had left the country for the duration.

Michael Foot – the Leader of the opposition – led the attack on a Government front bench that resembled a staff room of sulking teachers who had only just discovered their summer holiday had been cancelled. After the Prime Minister's statement, the Right Honourable member for Ebbw Vale repositioned his heavy black-framed spectacles for the umpteenth time and then rose to address the house.

'After the immensely popular public display of solidarity on Friday at Greenham Common, against the very real threat of nuclear war, the news of the expulsion of three KGB agents added to the catastrophic failure of the authorities to prevent a terrorist attack, the like of which we have never experienced in northern England and that has no equal in the history of the United Kingdom. Will the Prime Minister admit that her government is unable to adequately protect its own citizens and is losing control of events?' belched Foot, his white hair swinging dangerously over his notes.

The Prime Minister, Mrs Thatcher, responded by insisting that her government were the only administration that was capable of responding to the cowardly attacks from enemies both foreign and domestic and the leader of the opposition was more likely to be found holding hands with the likes of CND and appeasing insurrectionists than meeting the very real threat of terrorism when it raised its bloodstained hands. She was roundly cheered when she added that it was the Labour Party that had wanted to abandon the population of the Falkland Islands when faced with the invasion by the army of a fascist dictatorship just last year. It was not a debate that was characterised by any good feelings on either side.

In its early evening bulletin after *Grandstand*– and before *The Dukes of Hazzard* – the BBC reported that the Labour leader had landed a body blow to the Government during the emergency recall debate in the House of Commons earlier that afternoon, but he had failed to offer up any credible response himself. The MP for Whitborough, Sir George Shawcross MBE, gave a short speech paying tribute to the emergency services and the crew of HMS *Brazen* and pledging his support for the Prime Minister, sitting down to wide applause and the sympathy of his fellow backbenchers.

ITN's early evening news programme was postponed, and substituted for an old episode of *Chips*. After an announcement promising an extended *News at Ten*, BBC2 appealed for calm and national unity by continuing its coverage of the *Embassy World Snooker* semi-finals at the Crucible in Sheffield. Channel 4 showed Merseyside's idea of domestic bliss by running an extended *Brookside*, while its programmers argued about what to do in response to the other three channels' coverage of events, as they were unable to assemble enough senior members of the board. In the absence of the Chairman, Chief Executive and Head of Programming, the other board members chose to continue with their original schedule; the documentary on the predatory behaviour of great white sharks, followed by *Prisoner, Cell Block H*.

The concourse at Carr Wold Parkway had not welcomed so many reporters and cameramen since Cliff Richard's visit

17

to promote his starring role in the classic film *Summer Holiday* in the early 1960s. Every national and regional broadcaster and newspaper team had despatched a team to report on the attacks and the aftermath and record the response of the authorities. A scrum had developed in front of the portable stage and lectern that had been assembled hastily an hour before, in expectation of an announcement that was not yet forthcoming, though the throng of broadcasters and scribes were confident that must surely come in time for the BBC and ITN to file their reports for the main evening news programmes, at 9pm and 10pm respectively.

Superintendent Ascoyne d'Ascoyne – the most senior police officer in the borough, floated serenely over the concrete pedestrian crossing pontoon, at the Parkway's front entrance at 2pm in his chauffeur-driven Rover 3500SE SD1, wearing his best dress uniform for the benefit of the television crews. A brown leather document wallet, containing the text of a press release, faxed over from headquarters in Northallerton, rested on his lap. His driver steered the huge saloon into a coned-off area beyond the division's recovery truck to screen them from prying eyes. They were quickly surrounded by a throng of uniformed officers and two motorcycle patrolmen.

'Give me some space please,' demanded their commander, after smoothing down the front of his uniform. 'I'm here to make a short statement,' he announced, attempting to instruct his troops from the back seat of his car, 'then I'll be leaving immediately afterwards to meet the Chief Constable at Northallerton and some gentlemen from the Security Service in London. Where's Inspector Marshall?' he asked, addressing the nearest torso which was resting disrespectfully against the side of his car.

'What's that sir?' said one of the patrolmen, ducking down to the level of the window.

'Where's Marshall?'

'He's with forensics sir, in the pampas grass.'

'Right – stand back– I'm getting out!'

'Inspector Marshall and DS Broadhead are walking around the outside edge of the perimeter, with the dog team and forensics sir,'added Sergeant Moyne, avoiding the swing of the Rover's passenger door and feigning a curtsy, while the superintendent extracted himself from the back seat of his car, with as much dignity as the dimensions of the rear door aperture allowed.

'Has anyone spoken to those reporters?'enquired d'Ascoyne, once he had gained enough space to make his address and secure the attention of his officers.

'No sir,' came the collective reply.

'Sergeant Moyne?'

'Yes sir?'

'Be good enough to inform the ladies and gentlemen of the press that I will be making a statement within the next few minutes. But, I will not be taking any questions at this time. You may also inform them that the Chief Constable is appearing live on *Look North* tomorrow evening, for a twenty-minute question and answer session with their main anchorman. After that, all local newspapers, radio stations and regional television news organisations will receive a press release from Northallerton. No one will be making individual statements. That's all.'

'Yes sir.'

'Moyne?'

'Sir?'

'Before you address anyone, straighten your tie and collar and sort your tunic out, you're representing my station. I'll not allow my staff to be mocked because some of you look like you've slept in your uniforms.'

'As you wish sir,' he said impudently.

'It's not a wish – it's an instruction,' replied his superior acidly.

'Straight away sir!' replied the sergeant, making a deliberate show of himself, with a clumsy lunge through the two packed ranks of his peers on his way to the Parkway's toilet block, where he hoped to find a mirror in which to adjust the line of his uniform.

Meanwhile, in the shelter of a clump of tall grasses, Inspector Marshall and Detective Sergeant Broadhead were bending over a member of the police forensics team, who was carefully removing evidence from a small patch of flattened grass with some tweezers, tapping the sample gently into a clear plastic evidence bag.

'So what have we got Eric?'

'Well, this is where your terrorist was, Ray,' explained Eric Walker, the head of the forensics team. The grass is flattened here, where our man lay down and got into position. We've even got the bipod indentation marks from the machine gun further up, here… and here,' he added, pointing to two small pits around three feet beyond the patch of flat grass.

'Do you see these unusual dents in the turf inside the flattened patch of grass?' he asked, indicating a cluster of sharp indents in the ground, using his biro as a pointer. 'I was wondering what these might be. They're quite well-defined. Then I recalled the gunman was reported as having escaped on a motorcycle. I think these marks are the imprint of zip tags, from a motorbike jacket.'

'Mmm. That confirms the witness reports from the motorcycle showroom staff and the waitress in the Four Horsemen. Is that burnt cardboard?' asked Marshall, focusing on some fire-blackened scraps of ash beyond the crushed turf.

'Well, at first glance it does look like burnt cardboard. I've got a sample for analysis, just in case it's connected to our shooter. There's some crisp shards too. Cheese 'n' onion.'

'Cheese 'n' onion? How d'you know that!' said Marshall, amazed and outraged in equal measure.

'Here – smell this…' replied Eric, offering Inspector Marshall a small shard of crispy potato.'

'The bastard!'spat DS Broadhead.

'Yes, he's certainly one of those George,' concurred Marshall.'I hope this doesn't get in the papers. They'll have a bloody field day. Can you imagine the bloody headlines? *The cheese and onion shootout…*'

'Moving off the subject of crisps, that empty miniature bottle on the far bank you found might give us something Ray,' added Walker, 'and it might give you a line of enquiry too. Having the price tag with the name of the off licence is a bit of luck. I'm sure you can find out where the shop is. Tor Wines and Spirits – could be from Devon or Cornwall.'

'I'd put my money on Glastonbury,' said Broadhead.

'Leave some of those crisp crumbs for me would you Eric? Glastonbury! That's Somerset isn't it George?' added Marshall, scratching his neck.

'It could mean our man is one of those types that goes to those music festivals,' suggested Broadhead, thinking aloud. 'When he isn't trying to mow down people like us – obviously.'

'Aren't those things held in the summer?' asked the forensics officer.

'That's a point of view I hadn't considered. Well done George,' said Marshall thoughtfully. 'A good cover for an IRA assassin. Or – we could have ourselves a terrorist who tows a caravan. There must be what, at least ten camping sites around here, within five miles… sorry Eric– what did you say?'

'The Glastonbury Festival is in June, Inspector.'

'Mr Walker's right Ray. As for the camping sites…there'll be at least ten sir,' replied Broadhead; 'a lot of them hippies and dropouts that go to these things have caravans and old buses too. Glastonbury town's a hotbed of alternative culture all year round. Me and the wife had a couple of days there on the way to St. Ives. I've never seen so many hippies since I went to Reading to see Thin Lizzy.'

'She one of your girlfriends was she?' asked Marshall, teasing his friend.

'No, they're a rock band guv.' And the singer's Irish, but don't read anything into that.'

'Oh! I stand corrected,' replied Marshall, self-mockingly.

'Well, I've got what *I need* now Ray,' said Walker, struggling to get himself off his knees. You and George are welcome to lick the plates.'

'It's a *shame* you only found *three* of those bloody cartridge cases Eric. *Such a shame,*' said Marshall, looking Walker right in the eye before winking, then flicking his gaze at the ground.

'Ah….,' replied the forensics officer, understanding the implied request. 'Well, it was good to see you and George

22

again,' added Eric, jovially, letting a single brass bullet jacket from the crime scene fall out of his evidence bag. 'I suppose I'd better get back and get these booked in and sent out.'

'Before you go, Eric – just a second… sorry. George?'

'Guv?'

'Get us a couple of teas from the moby', he whispered, 'my mouth's as dry as an Ethiopian football pitch.'

'Sorry Eric – I just wanted to pick your brains.'

'Oh very laconic.'

'Promise I won't pinch your tweezers.'

'That's all right – I unwrap a new pair for each case; as you well know.'

'I wanted to ask you if it's worth doing a spot test on the bullet holes,' he said, nodding towards the crisp black skeletons of the Vauxhall Astra and the BMW patrol bike. Because the fires were quite intense, some of the tarmac melted under the car.'

'There's no possibility of me getting a trace metal sample from a spot test after a fire like that Ray. I can tell you that just by looking at them. So forget it. But we do have a shell case – *or two,'* he added coyly.

'Thank you for that.'

'Just before we go down that road, I wanted to clarify something. I know this is already being talked up as the work of some rabid new IRA faction. I'm not certain that's the case – would you like me to elaborate?'

'By all means do.'

'Well, most of the weapons that reach the Irish Republic and the north are usually manufactured in Russia, Yugoslavia and China. This bullet was made in Germany, at least forty years ago. You can tell by the patina of the shell case and the stamp on the bottom, which is rather a giveaway. So, what we're looking for is a World War Two machine gun. Although terrorists will use these things when they can find them, they're quite rare now and it's not going to complement the narrative which is about to be presented to the press by...'

'Superintendent d'Ascoyne?'

'A very self-confident man...' noted Walker, without any warmth.

'I appreciate the sentiment. Would you do me a favour Eric?'

'I'll consider it.'

'I know you're under a bit of pressure from on high, but I'd be very grateful if you could keep shtum, before the usual interval?' At a mutually agreeable time? That might even be after our superiors have established the likely perpetrators, independently of what you think of course,' said Marshall, not wanting to interrupt his superiors whilst they were intent on pursuing a fruitless line of enquiry.

'I like your train of thought... shall we see what transpires?'

'I couldn't wish for better...'grinned Marshall, tossing a coin in the air and catching it on the back of his hand.

'Oh just one other thing... I found a few strands of hair, the odd thing is, it's long and coloured. I'm going to test it for powder residue.'

'So it could have been a woman!'

'Well if it was, she doesn't have a very good hairdresser; the strands I found were blonde at the roots, fading into orange and red at the tips. She must be something to see.'

'Well there can't be too many birds with hair like that in Whitborough, thank you very much Eric.'

Hector Oliveras Morales, the owner of the Four Horsemen Mexican Cantina at Carr Wold Parkway, made the most ferociously hot chilli sauce in the county. In truth, it was probably the most dangerous substance that was legally available to the taste buds of the population of northern England. His restaurant's own Four Horsemen branded sauce was good enough to repel ants and cockroaches from his kitchen as effectively as a watering can of caustic soda. Their mule kick dip, Dia de los Muertos (Day of the Dead) bottled sauce and Ghost Chilli Salsa were potentially even more deadly to anyone with an above average sensitivity to spicy food.

Fortunately, these popular but 'challenging' condiments were always served with their own antidote – Hector's own recipe full fat banana milkshake, blended with cucumber and peppermint, mixed with single cream and runny honey, though his insurers had also insisted on the purchase of a portable defibrillator in order to minimise the risk that one of his famous dips might actually cause one of his future customers to expire. Yet, the Four Horsemen was still one of the favoured rest stops with Whitborough's traffic patrolmen, paramedics and ambulance drivers and the rival AA and RAC recovery teams, who used the Parkway as their unofficial base of operations.

The restaurant was colourful and cheerful inside, in the way of good traditional Hispanic cantinas– clean, and reasonably cheap. But it was the quality of the food that made them so popular, some of the best available anywhere on the A64. Together with his wife Maria and his sons Jesus, Cesar and Pablo and daughter Lela, Hector kept the businesses and visitors of the Parkway healthy and regular.

Before the arrival of the press, they were anticipating another average kind of day, or at least the closest one comes to an average day, after being the front seat witnesses to a terrorist attack. Although the walls of the cantina were studded with Spencer and Winchester rifles, naval Colts, Derringers and Colt 45s, the possibility of a real gunfight occurring on the concourse outside had seemed as remote as the country which they had left. Since the attack on the police, Hector had become impossibly proud of their role in the drama and was even considering a change of name for the restaurant that better reflected its new notoriety and frontier town status.

Maria his wife, unimpressed with the bullet hole scars and the crowds outside, was looking for an excuse to start an argument, bored with the Sunday food ingredients audit she was compelled to perform.

'Heyyyctor honey – you need send Cesar, to go to wholesaler before afternoon close. For milk and bananas – and cream. We have TWO! ONLY TWO CREAM CARTON LEYFT! All the big men they dreeenk last night.'

'Where is Cesar Maria?'

'Oh!… I send him lavatory… I cannot send Lela in after Rugby Club men use. Is no nice… they peece on floor like donkeys.'

'I will send Jesus to help when he is free.'

'Last night, they steal two menu – no, *threee* menu and warning sleeps last night. And all warning sleeps in others.'

'Maria, did you put new sleeps in?'

'No more sleeps in office, Heyctor. I say to Tina – yesterday, you breeng more. Now… she say she sick, she no come to work. I no put sleeps in you know anyway Hector – for waitress to do. Anyway… she no here.

'Then you collect tomorrow Maria, I tell you when we close last night I put new sleeps out, I ask you to tell Tina and Lela. You no remember!'

'I go to hairdresser in *moooorning* Heyyctorrrr.'

'No…YOU go to *PRINTSHOP FIRST!'*

'Okay, is okay, I make time…'

'Thee last sleeps, thee ones I leave out this morning, you tell Lela put them in the menus?'

'Where you put?'

'Ugh… that doesn't feel good,'grumbled Sergeant Moyne, adjusting his deportment in the mirror of the old bus station toilet. The sudden grumble in his intestines was the first warning of an approaching eruption for which there was no antidote or escape. Then a great wind of methane thundered down the track of his colon and burst forth from his sphincter, trumpeting its arrival with a forceful note in the key of G.

'Where is that bloody man?' muttered Superintendent d'Ascoyne, over the heads of his constables.

'Inspector Marshall is just coming down the bank behind you sir, from the pampas.'

'Not Marshall– Sergeant Moyne!'

'Sorry sir. He went to the toilet block to straighten his tie.'

'Well has he come out?'

'I don't know sir.'

'Well find out – now! I want the press quiet and docile before I read the statement.'

'Sir! I think I might have to use the loo myself actually. If you'll excuse me sir.'

'Hurry up Steadman.'

27

'Lela? How many police you serve?'

'All of theym… I theenk, Mama. They have wraps and tacos.'

'They have salsa?'

'Some of theym I theenk. I have to top up salad and salsa trays after they go away to pick-up truck.'

'You see new sleeeps Heyctor leave?'

'They were in the menus last night Mama.'

'No, you no understand – rugby club player steal them. We leave for you new ones to put in menus… you no put in menus?'

'No one tell *meee.*'

Marshall and Broadhead now rejoined the rest of their colleagues, having completed their sweep of the crime scene and the surrounding area. Their arrival did not put Superintendent d'Ascoyne in the best of moods.

'We seem to be missing a few people sir,' said Marshall bumptiously, striding silkily into the orbit of his superior with his dry companion in crime DS Broadhead, showing off their large polystyrene cups of tea.'Have they gone AWOL?'

'I beg your pardon?' replied the superintendent stiffly, uncomfortable with Marshall hovering at his elbow, cracking terrible jokes in his charity shop clothes, so close to the eyes of the press.

'AWOL sir. Absent without leave sir… Missing *without consent…'*

'Most of them seem to have been overcome by a sudden urge to inspect the toilet block,' sighed d'Ascoyne, ignoring the provocation.'They go in, but they don't come back out.'

'Is there something I should know sir?'

'I don't know – you tell me. I'm not privy to gossip, I've much more important things on my mind Marshall. Don't you have something else you can put on for the cameras?' scowled d'Ascoyne disapprovingly as he risked a glance at Marshall's trousers. It's not becoming of an inspector to look like he can't afford a decent set of clothes.'

'I wouldn't have found out half the things I have sir, if the people I met didn't think I was beneath them. Psychology is a very useful tool in police work sir. My wardrobe enables me to move through the world unnoticed – at one with the population,' said Marshall, enjoying himself.

'I know very well what psychology means, Inspector, but it might help us all if you'd carry another coat and hat, something smart for the media – when it's required. Is that really too much to ask? I think not.'

'Golf sir?'

'What?'

'Was that the other thing you had on your mind sir? Or should I say the Chief Constable's golf course discussion group. Career death that is sir…'

'Whilst we may have meetings there, what is actually on our minds is the protection, wellbeing and advancement of the service, Inspector. Where this is discussed between myself and my superiors is immaterial. Moreover, it's out of my control. What do you mean by career death for goodness' sake, you do talk rubbish sometimes Marshall…'

'Career death – *only seen at Christmas parties sir,* as they say in the Federation.Where would you choose to meet the Chief Constable sir, if it was up to you? There's plenty of nice little caffs with cracking sea views dotted about,' added Marshall mischievously.

'Why on earth are they still in that damn toilet block?' grumbled d'Ascoyne, studiously avoiding the little digs from his rebellious inspector, in an attempt to soothe the nervous tension behind the smooth, authoritative profile he was trying to project for his imminent appointment with the press.

'Elland, go and fetch our strays from the toilet block, there's a good chap,'snapped Marshall.

'Yes sir, Mr Marshall.'

'Inspector Marshall, son,' replied Marshall, speaking as a teacher chastising a rebellious child. Don't fret lad, I'm not mortally offended, but you need to get these little details right. You might upset Mr d'Ascoyne.'

'Sorry sir. Superintendent d'Ascoyne sir.'

'Superintendent d'Ascoyne,' repeated Marshall slowly and sarcastically, fixing Elland with a loaded stare.'Aren't you supposed to be somewhere else, Constable?'

'Sir?'

'Go and get yer mates out of the bloody toilet block,' yelled Marshall roughly, 'hurry up!' Elland turned around muttering, then started to run towards the cantina, until he was pulled up by the voice of his nemesis.

'Just a minute Elland,' called Marshall, toying with his awkward underling like a child trying to break an elastic band. Elland obediently returned to his tormentor, the inspector, who had a lollipop stick stuck in the corner of his mouth.

'Before you rush off in search of burping bums and the Andrex puppy Elland, has anyone been to the cantina before Mr Walker and forensics got here?'

PC Elland hesitated, then decided to confess, before the foundations of goodwill he had built up with his superiors over his short career disappeared in a cloud of methane.

'We were a bit peckish sir, so we ordered some wraps and tacos to take out.'

'What, *all of you?*'

'Everyone except Sergeant Moyne sir.'

'Oh?'

'He said he didn't want anything sir, though he ate my salsa – it were a bit too spicy for me.'

'He had a milkshake as well, did he Constable, like the rest of you?' asked Marshall, speaking as a man who had tried almost everything on the menu, except the pan-fried rattlesnake steak and the crispy tarantula legs.

'Milkshake sir?'

'Would you mind telling me what's going on – if you'd be so kind,' asked the superintendent.

'When you eat *anything* at Hector's, son,' snapped Marshall, speaking directly at the constable and ignoring his superior, 'you have to sign the bit of paper in the menu, the "get out of jail free card" that absolves Hector and his little family from any harm you may do to yourself, consuming their bloody condiments. If you've all done that, you'll know you need to order a milkshake with most of it. Don't tell me you lot have had the tacos, without ordering the bloody shake?'

'We just had the food as it was sir. Well some of it, anyway. Most of us never finished it. Is it too late to get one now?' he asked, beginning to worry.

'I'm surprised you didn't realise it was too bloody hot to eat as it was – you numpty!'

'We all had a cold drink sir, but it didn't seem to make a difference.'

'What did you swallow *on top of the food*– it wasn't fizzy was it..? Tell me it wasn't fizzy Elland…'

'Coke sir, the sergeant had two cans of Lilt. I had some Irn-Bru.'

'God almighty…'

Superintendent d'Ascoyne opened his mouth to speak, taking the air like a goldfish, then thought better of it and closed it again, fuming quietly to himself.

'Go and count the walking wounded in the toilets first. If you feel like you've got something brewing then stay near one of the closets. Off you go – don't worry, I won't call you back again,' said Marshall, reading the weary look of defeat on the face of the constable.

'Yes sir…'

'George?' said Marshall, turning to his number two.

'Guv?'

'Call the hospital and get them to send us a couple of ambulances. Tell them we're at the Four Horsemen, and we've got twelve cases of ghost chilli poisoning. Sorry sir,' said Marshall, belatedly meeting the eyes of his superior, 'you'll have to announce yourself this time unless you want to shove young Elland and his fart flute here on the stage as your opening act.'

'I trust you can handle things here?' replied d'Ascoyne, who was only too glad to have something else to take him away from the unfolding eruptions.

'A pleasure… as always sir. Say hello to the Chief for me, and apologise for the mix-up at the awards dinner last Christmas. I hope he's seen the funny side.'

Meanwhile, inside the Four Horsemen, Hector, Maria and Lela were holding forth over the cutlery and napkins station. Maria was still doing her best to rev up the atmosphere by fermenting a family argument.

'They eat tacos– and salsa– weethout milkshayke! You stoopeed girl, eez dangerous for theym!' They must sign a sleeep before they eat– so no comeback for us!'

'I'm not stupid Mama– nobody tell me we run out.'

'She's right Maria. Take a break outside Lela,– is all right,'said Hector, trying to calm his girl.

Meanwhile, in the toilet block, Sergeant Moyne, who had moved from the sinks into one of the two farthest toilet cubicles didn't know where to put his hands, though he certainly didn't want to move his feet, whilst his colon and anal trombone rushed to explore the full scope of their sound effects potential with the assistance of Hector's ghost chilli salsa and a litre of Lilt. Inside the limited privacy of the toilet cubicle, his ordeal was producing a cacophony of gurgles, rumbles and gaseous squeals that would have been hard to replicate anywhere outside the sound effects department at Broadcasting House. Inside his closet, lava bubbled, cabbage leaves foamed and trumpets, tubas and cornets traded blasts over deflating balloons, Christmas cracker whistles and porridge firing mortars.

In the opposite closet, Constable Steadman's sphincter was enduring an even greater baptism of fire and was close to collapsing completely; chapped and raw as it was, after passing a blast of steam and shit that could have stripped the paint from an armoured car. His legs and ankles had turned to jelly and he was now just one more fart away from going into shock and vomiting over his shoes. Two more victims, junior support staff from Northallerton press office were similarly afflicted, biting back their fingernails as their sphincters burst over their white enamel thrones, like Yellowstone Park mud geysers.

'Is there anyone else in here– that can get us some frigging toilet paper, please?'shouted Steadman angrily, noticing there was nothing in his closet to wipe clean his cheeks except the damp cardboard liner of the last toilet roll.

'Is that you Steadman?' groaned Moyne from the other side of the block.

'I'm gonna kill that bitch if I ever get out of here,'snarled the young PC, wishing he could put his fingers around the throat of Lela Morales before his intestines collapsed through his anus.

'There's five good dry rolls behind me on the cistern cupboard, I'll pass you one over,' shouted Moyne.

'It's not that friggin' Izal stuff is it Sarge?'

'No… it's powder blue, but in the circumstances, I don't really give a shit,' he groaned.

'Pink, orange or powder blue – I couldn't care less, just throw it over.'

'Here it comes lad…' shouted Moyne, throwing the roll over the top of his door. It soared gracefully over the gangway between the opposing closets and fell to earth inside PCSteadman's open air gas chamber. The policeman grabbed it with grateful reverence and started to uncoil a few feet of tissue paper to wipe away the evidence of his shame.

'Thanks Sarge, I owe you one– can you throw me another one over? I think I'm gonna need a few more sheets,'cried the constable, dabbing his watery eyes with his knuckles.

'Hi! Hello?'shouted an awkward, nervous young man in the closet beside Steadman. 'I'm out of paper in here too. Can you push me some over?'

'Can you lot hurry up in there!'called another voice, in the vicinity of the hand basins.

'Piss off, you cheeky bastard, can't you tell we're on the friggin throne!'shouted Moyne.

'Is that you Fergus?'

'Who wants to know?'asked the sergeant aggressively.

'It's Callum from the workshop. Are you gonna be much longer, we got some major gripes going on in the arse department Fergus.'

'Sorry Callum!'groaned Moyne apologetically, belatedly recognising the vocal signature of his favourite mechanic.'We're gonna be stuck in here for a while – can you get in the Little Chef?'

Colin Crawford – a staff journalist at the *York Evening Press* – observed the strained expressions and body language of the police with growing interest; from his third-class seat behind the barrier of the press and television crew enclosure. Reading the discord and friction within the ranks with a reporter's eye, his instincts told him that there was something very interesting unfolding, just out of earshot, that might become just as newsworthy as the story to which he had been sent to cover. So adopting an expression of tired impatience, he relinquished his place in the throng, backing out of the crowd of newspaper reporters and television people as slowly and patiently as he dared, rolling his eyes and smirking economically– feigning a dead leg limp, in front of his rivals to camouflage his escape. As the press of bodies thinned out towards the back of the scrum, he tucked his camera into his satchel and hid his press pass in his mac pocket. Then he made a slow circle round the side of the concourse, towards the toilets, looking for an access point to the toilet block through the fluttering bands of yellow tape.

With ten years under his belt as a staffer for the *London Evening Standard*, Crawford had realised the value of having a second identity when covering important stories. Over the space of a few years, he had assembled a hospital porter-style uniform, a fake ID and a gatefold invoice clipboard to pass himself off as a cleaning supplies delivery driver, in order to infiltrate restricted areas without arousing suspicion and fit in "behind the lines". It had worked like a dream, though he had had a few awkward encounters, changing his trousers around the rear doors of restaurants and hospitals, but his quick wit and persuasive patter had always saved him from what could have been an embarrassing trip to the police station.

Crawford slipped behind the back wall of the Four Horsemen into a gap between a stack of empty cardboard boxes, crates and waste food bins and began to change. Making sure he kept the cantina's rear doors in sight, whilst he swapped clothes, he checked the tiny cassette in his small dictating machine recorder, hiding his camera bag under a polystyrene fish tray lid.

Then he caught the sound of voices and boots running between the utilities building and the Parkway toilet block, next to the restaurant, so he checked left and right before attempting to move off and began to tip-toe his way along the edge of the bank – towards the noise of running feet.

Finding a convenient pile of stout delivery crates underneath one of the toilet blocks ventilation grilles, Crawford checked the vicinity again for any sign of a police presence and then clambered up the crate stack until he could hold his tiny cassette recorder against the rusted vent. There was certainly something interesting going on inside, as the volume of chatter had just taken a sharp upward turn, though Crawford still couldn't quite make out what was being said. So he stretched his arm to move the dictation recorder higher up over the grille cover and stepped on the foil-covered corner of the crate which had accidentally been smeared in sunflower oil. Leg followed foot, faster than a Bruce Lee drop kick, his arms flailing uselessly into thin air as he began to fall to earth, brilliantly mimicking the leaping form of the principal male dancer in *Swan Lake*. However Crawford's landing was much less graceful and certainly more gruesome, falling face down into the middle of the restaurant's waste skip onto a damp cardboard sheet, studded with heavy duty industrial staples over a pile of cheesy minced beef.

'Maria, you call doctor for men Lela serve. You see where they go, policemen who eat?'

'I see four meyn run in toilet block Hector.'

'Okay. You call Doctor – where you put kitchen rolls?'

Callum Tate ran out of the Parkway toilets with Detective Constable McCoy and PC Fincher, banging into the side of the food bin from which the tainted journalist was dismounting, knocking his dictation machine flying.

Crawford's escape from the waste food skip, in his sunflower oil smeared shoes wasn't going well. He had got into position for a dismount of sorts – on the inner lip – but as he tried to straighten his legs, the bin jerked sideways and he lost his balance for the second time in as many minutes. This time his luck ran out and he fell head first onto the hard asbestos soil pipe standing proud of the wall, behind the restaurant's staff toilet, knocking himself out.

Constable McCoy heard the crump and looked around the side of the bin, calling his colleague.

'Finch! Come ovver 'ere – quick.'

'What's the matter?'

'There's some blue collar bloke, looks like he's from a cleaning company unconscious behind the bins,' griped McCoy, crossing his legs.

'Any ID?'

'He's got some kind of badge on his lapel, but it's covered in bloody lasagne and cheese or something; check his pockets will ya Finch?'said McCoy.

The other policeman jerked the comatose journalist's trousers straight and put his hand into his right pocket, closing his grip on something that felt like a small misshapen leather pocket book and another article which had an altogether different texture and feel.

'There's a writing pad of some sort, and a– eeuurgh!'

'What's the matter?'

'There's a snotty tissue in there with it.'

'Pass me the wallet mate– *with your other hand…*'

'There you go – dirty bastard,' groaned Fincher, wiping his hands on Crawford's trouser leg. When he looked up again, McCoy gave him a filthy look.

'HIM! I meant him – not you.'

McCoy grunted and peered into Crawford's wallet, then tipped it upside down and shook out the contents over the comatose journalist's chest.

'He's alive is he?'

'Oh yeah – the bastard's still breathing.'

'Can you smell booze on him?'

'No. Nothing. He's not been drinking, he's been snooping

I reckon. No one's supposed to have been let through except the staff here. D'Ascoyne said we weren't allowed to let any delivery people past the tape… hang on…'

'There's a lot of plastic…'

'Colin Crawford – NUJ. National Union of Journalists.., the crafty bastard! Go and get Inspector Marshall…'

'Can you cuff him to the pipe? I really need the bog.'

'Go to Bol d'Or. You won't get in the Little Chef. *We've* occupied it.'

'They aren't gonna let me use their bog.'

'Flash your warrant card and say it's an emergency… go on then. I'll cuff this bugger then come back with Mr Marshall after I've been. The bastard's got a Socialist Worker membership card too. A bloody commie!'spat McCoy as his sphincter began to go into its first minor spasm. Fixing Crawford's wrist to a lug on the bin with his handcuffs as fast as he dared, DS McCoy stood up very gingerly and then ran towards the open garage workshop at Thunderbird Autos next door, whilst Fincher sprinted off to Bol d'Or Motorcycles.

'Police – I need to see your toilet. Where is it?' shouted McCoy, striding up to the first person he could find, waving his warrant card.'Detective Constable McCoy.'

'First door on the left – over there,' replied Adrian Coulter, their other mechanic, thrusting out a filthy arm from underneath a Corvette.

'Ta very much,' yelled McCoy, breaking into a jog as an enormous rumble thundered down his large intestine.

For the first time in his life, PC McCoy was delighted to find a filthy toilet with clean lavatory paper. There was certainly no danger that the throne of the swamp thing would be a greater threat to the health of the mechanics after his visit, than it had been before. Seizing the roll from the Swarfega-stained cistern cover, he began to tear off single sheets, overlapping them on the seat in a clockwise direction, then doubling back with more tissue, so he could have something, however thin, between the skin of his cheeks and the suspiciously stained black Bakelite. An old pattern hospital seat with a great gap at the front, so those unfortunates with a lot of overhang or bull-sized genitals could sit without having to squeeze their hoses inside the seat aperture. As soon as his tissue paper clock had covered the seat, he undid his trousers and bent down to the tainted porcelain. Nothing happened for the first few seconds and then a blast of methane burst forth from his quivering anus, causing ripples in the bacteria-infested water below. Then the churning torrent that had been building up behind erupted over the pan. Herb, the proprietor's adopted cistern spider, lost his footing in his haste to escape from the back of the toilet seat and fell in the deadly bristles of the toilet brush holder. McCoy sat sweating for a few more minutes then decided it was safe to stand. Trying not to look into the pan, he patted clean his anal water pistol, washed his hands with the brick of green soap and ran back to the rear of the Four Horsemen to reclaim his prisoner.

'Sir! Over here!'

Marshall and Broadhead strode towards the young Constable Fincher, taking a few last drags on the remains of their Benson and Hedges.

'Right! Where's everyone gone Fincher?' scowled Marshall. 'Are they all still on the bloody throne?'

'Callum and Norris from the car pound tried to get in the

toilet block sir, but the Sergeant's in there– with three of the others. McCoy had to use the mechanics' lav at Thunderbird Autos. I don't think they're going to be too fond of me at Bol d'Or.'

'Well you can buy them some bloody flowers if you've hurt their feelings can't you? What have you got for me?'

'We found a seventh columnist, I mean a communist – a journalist... passed out behind the toilet block. He's disguised himself as a cleaning company delivery driver sir...'

'Fifth columnists, communists, journalists and Seventh-day Adventists aren't hard to separate Fincher. You aren't going to get any higher than Detective Constable if you can't tell the bloody difference. Show me where the sod is...'

'I handcuffed him to the soil pipe behind the cantina sir.' I couldn't wait any...'

'Yes, yes. I bet you couldn't. We've all had one of *those* trips to the lavatory.'

A minute later, the three policemen were looming over the reporter's limp body. 'Here he is sir...'

'Well, well, well – it's Wolfie Smith Crawford, from the *Yorkshire Evening Press*,' grinned Marshall, pleased as punch. Did *you* empty his wallet like that Fincher?'

'No sir.'

'Well don't let me catch you leaving important evidence scattered over your next corpse like an upturned litter bin while you answer the call of nature again– you prat! RIGHT! Let's have a look through this twerp's card collection then.'Marshall bent down and picked up the Socialist Workers Party card, a communist party member's donor's chit and Crawford's NUJ identification card.

'Bag these up McCoy. And all his other bits,' said the

inspector, dropping the journalist's other cards and receipts back onto his cheese-smeared shirt. Have you checked the surrounding area yet?

'Didn't have time sir.'

'Bum before?'

'Er… yes sir'.

'Right – well if I know Crawford, he never forgets to take his camera and tape recorder to work, so have a root around until you find them. Fincher can help you when he's finished skiving. *This* sneaky little git was probably trying to embarrass us so we're going to pay him back– in kind. When you've got his camera and his tape recorder, you and Sergeant Broadhead can take him to the custody suite at the station and he can have the benefit of an interview with our "friends" from London, one lot, or the other. That'll teach the bastard to trespass on our crime scene.'

Chapter Five

Anarchy Mary

There was very little anarchy in Whitborough-on-Sea. Or indeed, any appetite or interest for anything resembling protest politics. The most important subject on most people's minds, after their family and friends, was money. Whether it was earned, made, stolen, spent or coveted. Money was the one thing no one could do without. The third position imperative, was whatever people did to forget about what they had to do to earn it.

Only a few lucky individuals of independent means were able to flourish outside the wage economy. Some had never had to join it. Mary Shipley Brown, the privileged daughter of a very astute stockbroker and private investor, was living comfortably in the second category, while carefully avoiding the first. Mary was young, driven and determined to make her mark in the world; even if Whitborough's citizens seemed determined to avoid her at all costs.

Mary's strident oratory continually frustrated her best efforts to keep an audience; repelling those in danger of being sucked into the gravitational pull of one of her ill-informed soap box rants– preposterous, ill-informed monologues and hectoring declarations that nimbly circumvented fact and truth, but were nonetheless still horribly compelling in their brutality and ignorance.

A finely indulged only child with a reasonable brain and good features, Mary had done what she could to make amends, adopting a lifestyle which made her look old at twenty. She smoked like Humphrey Bogart, drank like Richard Burton and trashed her hair so many times, she had been forced to give up bleaching and colouring for natural dreads. Allergic to real work and lacking any genuine charm or sense of humour, because of her all-consuming passion for protest politics, Mary had skilfully deferred her debut in the real world by becoming a perpetual student in the cosseted halls of Whitborough Technical College's art and design studios; living comfortably off her local education authority grant and monthly trust fund income, biding her time while she plotted her escape from provincial obscurity.

As the Whitborough town Labour Party and their unloved hangers-on in the Socialist Workers Party already had more than enough agitators of their own, Mary was compelled to force herself upon the only group of radicals left in the borough, that didn't have a Marx, a Lenin, or a Mao – the unfortunate young men and women of the Whitborough Anarchists and Vegan Collective, who were neither practising anarchists nor actual vegans by any reasonable definition, but a naive gang of boys and girls who were only really attracted to the recreational aspects of an alternative lifestyle drenched in cider.

The group 'occupied' a former Scout hut beside some abandoned allotments in Burniston, a short bus ride from the Technical College and fifty minutes' walk from town, the Scouts having moved to a brand new prefab within the Sea Cadets parade ground in Whitborough months before. Within two months of her arrival, Mary had declared herself General Secretary and Head of Propaganda, appointed a

Treasurer and Under Secretary and commissioned a banner and sign. Though her power grab ushered in a new chapter of seriousness that went against the spirit of the collective, they acquiesced, mostly, without a murmur, hoping she would tire of their indifference to her politicking, by making such a fool of herself that she would have to move on to the Bowls Club.

Disappointingly for Mary, one of the commune had arrived in Burniston late on Saturday afternoon with his new girlfriend, their new guest, a young lady who was about to show the rest of the group exactly how to put their Lagerfuhrer in her place.

The hut was winding down after a good-natured first encounter with the new girl, when Mary marched into view at the back of the facing sofa, directly in front of Mike and Aisha– his guest – remaining aloof and apart while she waited for one of Mike's friends to announce her.

'Oh sorry – this is Mary, Aisha, she's… Secretary… 'explained Stig, cocking his head in the direction of their leader before he turned his eyes towards his feet, muttering something which wasn't very polite. There was a palpable air of tension when Mary leaned forwards and threw out her hand. Aisha pushed herself halfway off the leather settee and reached out to grasp her fingers, though it felt as though she had just shaken hands with a mannequin.

Aisha tried to dispel the awkwardness, by smiling, but Mary had not come to exchange pleasantries. She was more concerned with discovering if their visitor was an infiltrator or a rival. A shy, modest and naive young guest would have warmed Mary's heart. But the person sitting opposite her was a very different kind of animal.

'Hi Mary, I'm Aisha – Mike's girlfriend. Allie says everyone here's veggie.'

'What?'

'Veggie.'

'So?'

'So… I'm like you. I'm a vegetarian.'

'You don't know nuthin''bout us or anyone. We ain't a club like that…' she harped, using obfuscation and rudeness in an effort to unbalance her guest. 'So… you're Mike's *newest* then,' smirked Mary, playing with her beads, 'most can't gel with us. We're too rad for most straights an' spare-time rebs. Not that you're a straight – I can see that. Has he told you the deal with us then, yeah? You wanna follow the band? You live like us.We gotta make up our own minds about newbies though. Groupthink, see. You squat?'

'Squat?… Sorry… I'm not sure I quite got your…'

'SQUAT? YOU SQUAT?'

'Mary, you can't interrogate someone you've only just met – cut it out!' groaned Gary who was slouched in a collapsed armchair beside the settees, picking his nose.

'No… I don't– *squat*. What's that got to do with anything?' replied Aisha, refusing to back down.

Mike covered his brow with his hand and groaned. Then Stig and Ian stood up and walked off, whispering amongst themselves. Aisha did her best to remain composed as she tried to defend herself without making a scene– so soon after her arrival. But she wasn't going to bite her lip for very much longer.

'You live with your mum and dad then?' asked Mary, more loudly than was necessary. Probing. Teasing.

'No. Actually, I share a flat with my sister.'

'Mary! Ease up yeah? The lass has only just got here,' said Digger irritably, jabbing the tip of his roll-up repetitively into the side of the old ashtray on their table top, but Mary ignored the intervention and pressed on without mercy.

'So you give money to a capitalist? A landlord?'

'That's usually how it works – *when you rent*,' Aisha replied, with carefully accented sarcasm.

Mary suddenly realised she had over-asserted herself and underestimated the quality of her opponent. But she couldn't back down and risk losing face in such an important duel, so she continued her attack in the hope she could quash the new girl's spirit before she got into her stride, though her luck was about to run out in the most dramatic fashion.

'You're perpetuating the capitalist system. That's oppressing the working class. None of us rent, we all squat. Checking your creds. Can't be one of us if you're part of the system. You got new docks…'

'I think you'll find Mike rents, don't you Mike?' replied Aisha coolly, glancing sideways at her boyfriend, who wasn't sure where to look, so he stared at his shoes and muttered an expletive under his breath.

'The flat belongs to my uncle, our *rents* are his only form of income– apart from his army pension. D'you think it's right we should sponge off him and leave him struggling for money, when he's been crippled, fighting to defend a free society and a free country like ours?'

'Ooooh… bull's-eye,' chortled Digger.

'That girl's got spunk. She's tough Benny,' said Cassandra, the bass player from the Card Cheats, enjoying the standoff from the safety of the next table. 'She's sticking it to Shipsulk. Go on girl.'

'Can't join us– if you got rels or famm in the services.'

'Rels? Famm? Rels means what? Relatives? Do you always talk in code and sneer at people you don't know? You are joking…'

'D'wee look like we're like that?'

'Pardon?'

'Pardon? Pardon? You ain't been to a compy… you go to a girls' school?'

'Leave it out Mary. Aisha's cool. She's one of us,' said Mike, fuming.

Mary sensed she was losing the room, and realised she had a finite amount of time in which to end the exchange, before her antics blew up in her face.

'She's got new docks!' She ain't one of us. She's a wage slave, and a Tory.'

'Mary! Cut it out,' growled Mike.

'She wants to infiltrate us…'

'I do not. What's wrong with having a job? I love my job. How can you be a rebel if you take handouts from a government that you claim to despise?'

'You ain't judging us.'

'Don't judge me then – and stop speaking to me in your stupid code. How dare you speak to me like some toxic headmistress. Are you always so rude and aggressive to people who are supposed to be your guests?'

'She's working for the system Digg. Listen to her, she's trying to diss me.'

'Mary. You went to a private school,' said Digger, exasperated by Mary's goading.

'Did not.'

'Did so.'

'Whitborough Girls' College isn't private. It's open to everyone…'

'Like everyone who can pay the fees? Listen… Aisha's sound. She works in the vet's on Gunstone.'

'Her Dad subs *her* hundreds every month…' complained Cassandra within earshot, adding to Mary's troubles.'Silly bitch.'

'C'mon Aisha…' said Mike angrily, as he got to his feet.'I'll get us another drink away from Punkerella.' But Aisha refused to budge. Mary, who had taken umbrage against one of her flock for mentioning her private education suddenly spotted Keith the drummer in the Card Cheats was eating a dead animal pie and chips. Her interrogation was not going as smoothly as she'd hoped.

'Mike, I'm not going anywhere, and I'm not running away from *her*,' she snapped, glaring at Mary.

Mary ignored her answer and went back on the attack, revisiting her critique of Aisha's choice of shoes, going for the moral high ground, as she perceived it, looking for a scalp and a quick victory. 'We don't wear leather, us or the band. Dead animal skins ain't where we're at. We're vegans. Hunt sabs. You can't wear them if you're around us.'

'So you tell people what they can wear, and who they can and can't mix with, do you Mary? Like some kind of creepy fascist social secretary?'

'WHOA!' gulped Digger. 'Shit's gonna hit the fan.'

'Mike didn't hear. He was transfixed with shock and admiration, waiting for the inevitable explosion. The rest of the witnesses were hurrying away to the margins of the Scout hut, avoiding eye contact with the two girls at the centre of the ideological stand-off, though still staying determinedly within earshot.

'Did you just call *ME* a FASCIST?' yelped Mary, blinking furiously, pressing her palm over a cleavage garlanded with the cheap, slag metal symbols of rebellion, hanging from loops of coloured string. 'How dare you call *ME* a FASCIST!' she shouted, almost popping her nose stud. '*Your* uncle was the servant of an imperialist fascist government and a warmongering bitch!' she announced to the room, pushing her head and shoulders into the space between the sofas.

The uppercut was very swift, and totally unexpected. The knuckles of Aisha's right hand, slammed into the defiant chin of her tormentor with a loud crack, felling the Queen of Whitborough's underground scene in a heap. For a long time nobody spoke or moved, then very quietly some of their audience began to whistle and clap.

'Don't bother getting up, unless you want the rest too,' said Aisha, standing over her groaning tormentor. My uncle fought to save more deserving people than you from being taken over by a real fascist state. Not that you'd know a real fascist, unless you got shot by one – you bitch. Or looked in a mirror. Oh, and by the way, we live in a democracy. That's why dickheads like you can walk the streets without getting locked up.'

'SHIT Aisha! WHAT DID YOU DO!' yelped Gary, trying not to laugh. Mary's hand slumped off her chest and flopped onto the floor.

'Something worthwhile. Wouldn't you say? I don't see anyone rushing to pick her up, do you? Just keep that bitch away from me from now on,' snapped Aisha, storming off to the toilet with a tissue pressed into the corner of her eye.

'Aisha! Where are you going – she might go to the cops!' shouted Mike, appealing to his fleeing girlfriend, then suddenly revised his last comment when he'd had a few seconds to think. 'Well, maybe not…'

'Can someone splash a bit of cold water on Shipsulk to wake her up,' suggested Digger, 'she's just passed out.'

'I'll go!' 'We'll go!' shouted three or four of the group in unison, falling over each other in their haste to grab the four red fire buckets from the brackets outside the main door and fill them up with freezing water.

Two of Mike's friends, Cheesy and Stig arrived over Mary's unconscious form, grinning sheepishly. 'D'you need some help to drag her outside? We can't soak 'er in 'ere, can we? We'd have to mop up.'

'Yeah, okay,' answered Mike, trying not to grin too broadly, 'd'you want to grab 'er arms? Me an'Aisha'ull grab 'er legs… when she comes back.'

'Aisha's gonna be in the bogs a while longer I reckon Mike,' said Gaz. 'Somehow, I don't think she'll want to touch her anyway. I'll give you a hand.'

'Better be nice then when she comes back, or she might deck one of us an' all. She's got a cracking punch. DIGG! Hold the door open for us mate.'

'She's gonna be pissed when she wakes up,' said Cheesy. 'She *was* gonna show us what she's been hiding under that old quilt cover, after us teas. I guess we won't get to see what she's been up to, unless we can wake her up.'

'Hasn't she told you then?'

'Told me what? You mean you know – already?'

'We're gonna liberate some donkeys tomorrow night.'

'DO WHAT?'

Chapter Six

North Yorkshire Police Headquarters, Northallerton

Superintendent d'Ascoyne's expected meeting with the Chief Constable of North Yorkshire Police was not the friendly one-to-one reunion that he had been anticipating. The actual format of their encounter, which was very different from the one he had envisaged, had done absolutely nothing to improve his mood. Instead of the informal chat he had hoped for, inside the comfortable surroundings of the Chief Constable's inner sanctum, with port and cigars, he found himself in a cold prefab on a hard plastic chair, facing the Assistant Chief Constable, his ice maiden secretary and two furtive-looking civilians or officials who looked as though they had been in the military all their lives and had now moved into some kind of Neverland between the Ministry of Defence and some shadowy department of state attached to the Home Office. They wore no identification or badges of rank, but were clearly overseeing and directing the meeting to which he had been summoned but not forewarned. It had all the hallmarks of a disciplinary inquiry without the safeguards or protocols which the service was usually so careful to observe.

The Assistant Chief Constable had already enraged d'Ascoyne by not doing him the courtesy of introducing their guests by name. His resentment was becoming harder to hide with each second that passed.

'This is a Home Office investigation, in partnership with the joint services, directed by the cabinet office,' explained the Assistant Chief Constable, finishing his statement with a grunt of distaste.

'Surely this is purely a police matter sir, until…'

'The Home Secretary has insisted upon the postponement of all meetings at Whitborough station *and* here at headquarters, pertaining to the sinking of HMS *Brazen*, until the arrival of liaison officers from the Home Office and the Royal Navy. The MOD are also sending two representatives from the Intelligence Services. You will afford these gentlemen full access to all areas of the station without exception, including your own office and the interview suites,' explained the Assistant Chief Constable tersely.

'But…'

'You will chair the meeting and ensure all the parties stay within the terms of reference set out in the document,' he added, placing the tips of his fingers on a manila folder at the front of the desk. 'There will be no recording devices allowed during these sessions – only written notes and minutes. Any non-operational staff they may require will give their full co-operation – after signing the Official Secrets Act, after which they will be required to maintain full confidentiality or face the full force of the law. You must clear three rooms at the station for a week from tomorrow. All senior officers based in Whitborough, must be at the station by 6am to receive an advance team of counter-intelligence specialists, who will perform an examination of each room, before sealing them. The first meeting will commence at 10am. I've not been given any more details other than these at the moment, d'Ascoyne.'

'Are we leading this investigation sir?'

'Of course, it is still a police matter.'

'Until it isn't.'

'*We…* will be given the courtesy of laying out our evidence and theories first,' emphasised his superior, managing not to catch the boring eyes of the sour-looking men to his sides, 'though as chair you have the freedom to appoint an officer of lower rank to present the facts while you read the room. What about Marshall? He's got a few years under his belt, we can't have anyone too gauche or green.'

'Marshall?'

'I know the two of you don't see eye to eye, but you'll have to put aside any personal rivalry and do your best by the service d'Ascoyne. The greater good.'

'Yes sir, but Marshall is just an inspector. He'll be presenting the most important case we're ever likely to deal with at the station, to a room full of people who do nothing except look for Russians, fifth columnists and terrorists.'

The two men on the extreme left and right of the Assistant Chief Constable looked into each other's eyes very briefly with a fluency that might easily have been missed– then broke off eye contact, returning their gaze to a point on the opposite wall just above d'Ascoyne's hat. It wasn't overtly demeaning to the man opposite them, but nor was it accidental. D'Ascoyne crossed his legs.

'And you'll be making sure we come across in the best possible light…'

Chapter Seven

Operation Donkey

Many miles away from Police Headquarters in Northallerton, where one meeting had just ended, the Burniston Anarchists Devolved Committee of Whitborough (BADCOW) had just convened and were gathered around the form of a mysterious protuberance hidden beneath a quilt cover on the old Scoutmaster's trestle table. Mary– now revived – stood behind the table, in front of her troops and then grasped the edge of her precious signs of the zodiac bed linen, lifting it off with great ceremony in the manner of a magician's assistant, once she had put aside her soothing bag of ice cubes.

On the table before them lay a strangely-shaped hummock of papier mâché that could have been mistaken for a giant green turd, were it not for an untidy ridge of mixed sized bristles that covered its summit like a badly-mown mohican. A small wire tower, made from coat hangers in the same style as the famous RKO broadcasting beacon, stood on the highest point at one end, next to a mustard-coloured obelisk on a cardboard plinth. A long ribbon of wet 'n' dry abrasive paper (representing a road) curled its way through the bristles in a giant loop, then ran down one side of the mound, looping around a group of small structures resembling a toilet block within a small paddock.

'Mary – did *you* make this?'asked Jim, one of the small

minority in the collective who stood up for Mary, when she was in danger of making a fool of herself.

'Yeah. I've been working on it at college,' replied Mary, sullenly, wincing slightly, as she pressed her bag of ice against the bruise on her chin. 'It's plaster and papier mâché, painted with gouache, mostly. I made the other bits at home.'

'Where's the railway, Mary?'

'Railway..? What railway?'

'There's no model railway…'

'Yeah, where are the tunnels Mary?'

'What!'

'There's no track or station or platform either.'

'What are you talking about? Can't you see what it is?'

'Is it one of them, them – Neo… Neo – lith… one o' them burial mound things?'

'They call 'em Barrows dunt they? I seen one o' them things once. On the telly, in Scotland. Or Orkney.'

'Bauhaus did that song about them – 'Hollow Hills'. Cool band Bauhaus.'

'It's Oliver's Mount!' groaned Mary. 'It's a scale model of Oliver's Mount. *There's* the television tower thingummy – *there's* the war memorial and *there's* the woods – an' the racetrack,' she snapped, pointing at each of her creations. 'I spent two months making this after lectures…!'

'What for?' asked Stig, with a look of bewilderment.

'What for? *WHAT FOR?* For OPERATION DONKEY – DUMBBELL!'

'But if we know where the donkeys are, why do we need a model railway… model?' said Ian impolitely.

'IT'S NOT A BLOODY MODEL RAILWAY!' croaked their Fuhrer, trying to ignore the pain in her swollen jaw.

56

'Calm down Shippie, you'll bust a tampon,' said Cassandra, attempting to cool down the tempo of the discussion.

'It's a scale model of the landscape – the terrain through which we will effect the rescue of these abused animals,' asserted Mary, trying not to register the taste of blood from her gums. 'By studying this model, we can pinpoint the route of our escape, avoid populated areas, and identify any hazards. We need a three-dimensional representation of the TZ and the MLP to plan our mission in detail, if we're going to do this properly. The *railway track* won't feature in the rescue operation; so there is no need to include it on the model.'

'She's thought this one through lads.'

'Mary?'

'Yes Digg?'

'What's a TZ?'

'It's on your handouts. You're sat on yours…'

'Right…'

'TZ means target zone Digg,' said Gary.

'MLP stands for *mission landscape platform* boys,' said Cassandra. '*Not* my large penis.'

'It's a good job Mike and Aisha's gone. This shit wouldn't 'ave got out the pram,' whispered Ian to Penny beside him. 'She works at the vet's on Gunstone. They look after a lot of horses and donkeys; she'd soon shut this daft cow down.'

'That silly cow's not getting me mixed up in this. It's got disaster written all over it…'griped Penny.'Why doesn't someone call her out?'

'Coz we're all waiting for her to fall off her high horse – and run home, to Mummy and Daddy,' hissed Cassandra.

'No whispering in the Ops room!'snapped Mary. 'I will

now present to you all the plan for Operation Donkey; after the briefing I'll be happy to answer any questions. Until then – please remain silent.'

'She's crackers.'

'It's like the start of *Where Eagles Dare* in that scene in the war office in London innit?' grinned Ian, remembering his favourite war film.

'Aye. Ours is the low budget Yorkshire version –*Where Donkeys Fart.*'

'What's that funny lump, in the green fuzzy bit, by the war memorial Ship?' asked Badger, who was also at the same college as Mary, doing Business Studies.

'It's a teaspoon, Badge. It got stuck in the plaster okay – forget about that. The bristles represent the trees – the wood. *This* is the donkey paddock,'said Mary, pointing to a cardboard wristwatch box, to which she had added a roof made of overlapping paper scales.

'Prison.'

'…Prison then.'

'It's a matchbox innit?'

'Stig. Keep up mate. It's a model,' said Ian sarcastically.

'Don't lean on the Mere Stig, the tin foil might come off.'

'Soz Mary.'

'Right – everyone get where they can see,'ordered Mary, beckoning her anarchist commandos to the edge of the trestle table, until they were all squeezed in beside each other.

'Is this gonna take long, the pubs are open in 'alf an hour?'

'Ian, you're a soldier of the revolution,' said Mary earnestly.

'Yeah, sorry. Just looking forward to a few beers.'

'This has taken weeks of planning.'

'Soz Mary.'

'Just be quiet everybody and listen. Can everyone see now?'

Brian and Dave Drake decided to go for a Chinese takeaway on their way home to Bader Drive on the Neatsfield Estate, after a manic day at the shop.

'I thought that prat Phil Kennedy might have been in for his gear today. Are you gonna have Peking duck again?'

'Not tonight. I'll have the chicken curry and boiled rice. I need some stodge to soak up all the brandy coffee and the saturated fat from Corfe's caff. Did any of the others come in while I was at the library?' asked Brian wearily.

'Just the two bouncers from Mystery City. And Jocky from Vicky's. Dean says there was a big scrap inside the Orange Tree last night and someone clocked Kennedy. Might be why he's staying in until his black eye settles down, so he probably won't come around until late Monday.'

'Good.'

'How's the rhino book?'

'I don't know. I haven't had chance to look at it yet. I'll have a butcher's at bedtime.'

'Another two days of mayhem. Dean's done sixty LPs today – and we've sold all them picture discs.'

'And we've run out of Twisted Sister t-shirts?'

'Yep.'

'Shit…'

Chapter Eight

Boldwood's Excursion

The worst possible kind of light shone down through Lindsay Boldwood's bathroom window, just as he stepped into his steaming bath to pull the curtains aside and raise the sash window. Although the moon was now waning over Cloughton, Boldwood had already transformed for the first time – and could now bring on the wolf at will after sundown. His low mood could also cause the change subconsciously after too much stress, even as the moon waned – and he had had more than enough aggravation from his younger staff earlier in the day to start another night of carnage.

His skin began to prickle and darken suddenly as the virus rushed from its hiding place in the tiny gland behind his eyes, though at least on this particular night he was in the bath and not on the toilet, as he had been when it had first come upon him the previous Tuesday. Boldwood's flannel and duck were the first victims of his second hormonal eruption, torn to shreds by his soapy claws as the man-wolf tried to extract himself from the huge roll-top bath, nails skating in panic and rage on the slippery bubble-covered porcelain. Finally, a soaking wet werewolf flopped panting onto the bath mat and sniffed its slippers, then shook itself dry, growling at the Sooty and Sweep toilet roll covers as he approached the open sash once more. Through the gap between the bath and the wall, Boldwood climbed onto the sill, hesitated for a second on the window ledge then leapt down onto the arbour frame and crashed onto the roof of the love seat, from where he dropped down onto the decking. Two of the older single male guests who had been imbibing steadily since lunchtime saw him approach one of the tables where a tray of half-eaten prawn cocktails, sausage rolls and vol-au-vents had been abandoned.

'Hey Rab... have yee sheen hem ootseed? Ez that the beyst werewolf costume yew ever sheen... odd theng tee wear forra Lords an' Ladies neet,' remarked Nairn Thompson, glancing at Boldwood's haunches through their window onto the yard.

'Aye, therrs alluz one who'll tunn up eynn the wrong threads... Ah thenk yon fella shudd lose a few pounds eh? There's no gev by the sheams – ugly specimen, very real-essteck though.' Then Rab craned forwards, over the drop-leaf table by the windowsill, leaning on their cases to get a better view and stop himself from swaying too much, whilst he re-examined the form of Mr Boldwood through the old glass window panes... 'OH *SHITE!'*

Boldwood sniffed the food, but declined the seafood pastries. The aroma of meat juices had drifted into the yard from the open doors of the Crescent Moon takeaway a hundred yards away on Pilger Street, one of the smaller lanes off Cloughton High Street; the powerful scent, floating on the breeze from the great slab of lamb turning slowly in front of a grill, made Boldwood's coat prickle and he immediately broke into a run, chasing down the smell of the meat.

Upon reaching the back alley behind the kitchen,

Boldwood the beast slipped unseen through the open back gate. He sniffed the air cautiously, but his path to paradise was suddenly blocked when the dishwasher boy Aydin slammed the rear fire door shut, on his way to the fridge, just before the monster in the yard could leap inside. Puzzled by the ribbed steel sheet covering the door face, Boldwood turned his attention to the grate under the sink waste pipe and sniffed the iron drain cover, just as the chef poured a huge pan of boiled cabbage leaves into a mesh strainer over the sink.

Three gallons of bitter green boiling water burst violently over the drain, splashing Boldwood's nose and tongue. The roar from his agony caused the chef to let go of the pan handles of the rice pan and flee into the toilet in blind panic. Boldwood dashed out of the yard and ran into the fields at the back of the terrace, plunged his head in the brook to relieve his pain, then galloped off into the wood and onto the track to the old railway line to Whitby and Kettleness, guided by his knowledge of the landscape, and the dim recollections from boyhood memories of trips to Sandsend and Runswick Bay.

He was travelling quickly now, at least twice the speed of a thoroughbred racehorse, despite his bulk, driven by an urge to test the extent of his strength and endurance. He found that he was tireless and ran on, following the railway from higher ground, as it snaked its way around the contours of the moor on its path to Whitby. For miles he ran, keeping the track on his right as he headed north towards the coast until he came to the tower of Kettleness church, overlooking the narrow lane which led down to the two farms and the small group of cottages that sat before the cliffs. Boldwood stopped and sniffed the air, stalking the edge of the churchyard beside the boundary wall, taking care to stay downwind of his prey, a small flock of ewes and lambs on the edge of sleep in the next field. He found himself a spot downwind, just behind a thinned out section of hedge in a clump of reeds, concealed himself behind the foliage and waited.

Chapter Nine

Lords' and Ladies' Night

The Shirestones Hotel had always been full for the Easter Bank Holiday, for as long as anyone in Cloughton village could remember. It was the first of the many big paydays for the business, which began in the spring and finished with the Gold Cup Races at Oliver's Mount, at the end of September. Since Lindsay had taken over the freehold, he had started to sell the hotel to travel companies in the bigger Scottish towns and cities, the same businesses that took bookings for the traditional annual pilgrimage south that was known as Scots fortnight. His intention was to draw down some of the same crowd for the Easter holidays and save himself time and money by securing block bookings with the least amount of effort on his part. It had worked very well and left him time to concentrate on other matters.

To this end, Boldwood had decked out the hotel with bunting and flags to create a party atmosphere and organised three different themed nights for the Easter Weekend, in an attempt to keep his guests on site during the evening, to increase his takings. Good Friday and Easter Saturday were billed as Tarts and Vicars Night and Lords and Ladies Night respectively. Easter Sunday was billed as the Hawaii Five-0 Coconut Lounge Dance Night, with a short set by the

Bingley Beach Boys, a world-class tribute band from West Yorkshire who were booked at the Paul Murray Concert Hall in Whitborough later the same night.

Friday night had started promisingly, but thinned out a little, when a minibus arrived to whisk off some of the guests for a pub crawl in Whitby. But as soon as his regulars in the village arrived, their absence was barely noticed, until the remaining streetwalkers and priests disappeared in a small fleet of taxis after 9pm, driving off in the other direction after hearing about the fire on HMS *Brazen*, to go and gloat over the carnage. Saturday night was looking much better for Lindsay and the staff, though Boldwood had suddenly disappeared just as the buffet had finished. Fortunately, the hotel was in good hands and he was not immediately missed. The party was still in full swing when Boldwood (still on four legs) padded back into the hotel's rear yard covered in blood at 1am.

After an entree of lamb, followed by a prize cockerel and the savage dismemberment of two elderly ewes, Boldwood had wrapped up his murderous foray above Whitby with a main of Cycliste(s) sur Tente (al dente) x2. He also despatched a dog fox, which had hissed at him, as an impulse kill prior to his return. He was, in his own words, well and truly stuffed when he returned home in the form of his supernatural alter ego, with no room or appetite for anything bigger than a Pepperami or, indeed, a wafer-thin piece of Yorkshire Terrier. As a man, his attitude to food was to be opportunistic when it was freely available, but frugal when it was something that needed to be bought, an attitude he carried over into the wolf. So when he came across one of his guest's tiny dogs – tied up, and waiting patiently opposite the men's for its master –

he opened his jaws and advanced for one last bite. Then the toilet door swung open and the man mountain of Glaswegian shipbuilding that was Robert Cunncliffe emerged from the washroom.

What he saw in front of him was the last thing he had expected to see in a hotel corridor in Yorkshire or anywhere else. Wolves he *had* seen, not in first floor hotel corridors, or anywhere else in a domestic setting. A wolf bigger than a fully-grown male lion was a completely different kettle of fish, though Mr Cunncliffe didn't dwell too much on the scene. His dog was in danger and he wasn't the type of person who had ever been a bystander in an emergency or a fight. Cunncliffe looked about for a weapon, saw a suitable object, then stepped carefully to the blind side of the gigantic predator which appeared to be about to pounce, seizing one of Boldwood's stout antique warming pans, conveniently situated on a filigree ironwork bracket below the picture rail, just within reach.

Boldwood never heard the vicious-looking iron pan head, as it swept down onto his shaggy shoulder blades with all the force the mighty Scotsman could muster, shattering his spine, with a noise like a box of hazelnuts being crushed under a pallet of bricks. His chin hit the carpet with a loud thud. Cunncliffe added a second blow to his spinal cord, as severe as the first, then jumped on his skull and scooped up his trembling pet.

Worried he had over-reacted and mortally injured the thing rolling in agony on the rug, Cunncliffe checked the other doors on the landing were still shut, then ran clumsily up the staircase before anyone who was sober came into view.

Bruised, battered and badly constipated, Boldwood

squirmed and whimpered in anguish until his injuries began to heal. Then he limped up the royal blue Axminster-shod stairs from the function room corridor, just as the conga was joined down below at the Lords and Ladies disco. Behind the curtains and the glass partition, lights flashed and twirled, knees jerked and legs kicked as the half-cut train of Caledonian revellers hopped and jigged to the happy trumpets and bongo beats of Modern Romance's 'Best Days of Our Lives'.

Boldwood the werewolf could stand no more. Squatting on his thick muscular haunches beside the telephone table on the second floor near his rooms, the landlord clenched his teeth and squeezed, using his abdominal and pelvic muscles to best effect, forcing an enormous compacted stool of human and animal remains to the eye of his anus. Foul clouds of gas hissed past the swollen walls of his sphincter and the foul turd which had just reached the end of its journey shot from his haunches like a party streamer, accompanied by a great splash of blood slurry and semi-digested fox, just as Kid Creole's apologetic hymn to mistaken paternity broke out from the speaker cabinets. Boldwood, now saggy-legged, but free of his tormenting blockage, began to shrink back into human form.

Chapter Ten

The Spy in the Cab

Two smartly-dressed, broad-shouldered men with tough faces, carrying identical briefcases, boarded the first-class compartment of the 08.55 express to Edinburgh, from platform ten at King's Cross Station, on the Sunday morning of the Bank Holiday weekend and took a reserved compartment in the middle of the car. Neither man spoke, until they had locked the door to their compartment. The older man, who appeared to be in his late forties, was wearing clothes of a slightly better cut, a stone Barbour mac, a vanilla shirt, Burberry tie and a mid-brown three-piece suit with Gladstone boots. The younger man was dressed in a navy Burton mac and a blue pinstripe suit, a light blue shirt, RAF tie and black Air Force-style shoes with shorter hair. He remained standing, lingering by the window onto the narrow corridor outside their partition, whilst the older man sat down and brought out a key from his pocket to unlock the padlock holding the links of a silk-covered chain to his wrist.

'If the corridor's clear Bruce, you can do the sweep now. Draw the curtains first.'

'It's two hours thirty minutes to York is it?' asked the younger MI5 officer as he carefully checked the upholstery, trim and fittings in their compartment for bugs of the electronic variety.

'One stop at Peterborough.'

Several minutes passed before the younger man paused and turned to his colleague.

'Nothing in here with us sir. Looks like the RMT/KGB stooge didn't get wind of us.'

'Perhaps the bastard is having a sickie– if he's seen the news this morning. Control said the BBC and ITV breakfast shows were going to run the announcement about the three expulsions today. Make sure you go outside to show the ticket inspector our stubs when he comes. Don't let *anyone* in here until we get to York,' said the older man. 'Not even the Secretary of State for Defence. Now switch this on, and put it on the seat beside you,' he said, handing his colleague a portable radio jammer. 'We can use this one at the B&B too, because we won't be watching the TV in our room either.'

'How many days have they given us up there – if we can get a bloody room?'

'It's a discretionary. Open-ended for MACE assignments. Don't worry about the room, that's the beauty of working for the Intelligence Services, we get to go where no one else can.'

'MACE, sir?'

'Mass casualty events committee. It's only fallen between our section and theirs because the victims were 50/50 civilians and MOD personnel. There's a sub-committee in the service that meets to discuss "*the detection and prevention of*". This business seems to have caught the committee by surprise, which is why it's been expanded – to spread the blame. Rule number one, on assignment: don't be left without the best girl's telephone number if the music stops. If we don't find the hands that held the smoking gun in Whitborough-on-Sea, then we're shafted. We are now MACE-affiliated Ops agents. However, there is some good news, we've been shunted two bands higher on the pay scale, which is permanent and irreversible – even if we fall into the back offices without so much as a fingerprint. It's compensation– for career death, which is permanent secondment to translation duties to you and me. Personally, I'd prefer a discharge to listening to hours of small talk from a bedsitter in Prague. But that's the worst that'll happen.'

'Oh wonderful! That's just what I've been waiting to hear…'

'No need to be fatalistic yet. We've got a couple of nights' bed and breakfast initially. Rooms with a sea view, in a guest house called Bronte's Rest on Long Acre. It's near the castle, apparently; run by a chap who's been in RAF intelligence. There's plenty of tracks and paths around the castle's dykes and flanks, so you'll be able to make the most of all the fresh air when you go out for your morning constitutional. If it's not up to scratch we've got plenty of time to look for something more convivial. But it looks very nice on the leaflet they sent. Some small compensation for our trouble.'

'They don't take tradesmen at Bronte's Rest do they?'

'No.'

'Thank goodness for that. I don't want another night like the one in Douglas.'

'Well that Libyan gun runner you put in the spirit world won't be giving his neighbours any trouble for a while. It's amazing what you can do with a cheap umbrella and the right sort of training. I can still see the look of agony on his face when you broke the spindle cog, slamming it past his tonsils.'

'Do you know what I hate about Yorkshiremen?'

'I didn't realise you'd spent enough time there to develop such strong opinions on the inhabitants,'said Stocke, the senior man, looking at the ingrained dirt and nicotine-stained windows with disgust.

'You'd feel the same if you'd had three years at Leeds University. They're not a pleasant race, in the main. I've never met one that didn't try and bulldoze me into silence and awe with their own half-baked opinions. It doesn't matter what you happen to be talking about, you've got to hear what they think about it first. And the women are worse than the men. Before you've even got a conversation out of the front gate their mouths are open. They just love the sound of their own prattle.'

'Really? Well.., if the police fit the pattern, then at least we should have a meaningful discussion. I was more concerned it was going to be one-sided, like these things usually are. I don't know why we have such a terrible effect on people. As soon as someone I'm at ease with finds out I work for the Security Service, the conversation dries up faster than a sultana in a pizza oven – and they suddenly remember they've got to be somewhere else; or they develop a sudden speech impediment. It's almost like they can see horns breaking out through the skin on your brow.'

'Good God, people don't put sultanas on pizzas now do they? I know tastes have changed since I was an undergraduate, but I don't remember being able to buy a pizza with bloody currants on top.'

'Sultanas…'

'Sultanas, currants, isn't one just a larger version of the other?

71

'Bruce, I wasn't suggesting anyone puts sultanas on pizzas. It was just a metaphor. Can we get off the subject?'

'Oh…'

'I always say… it would help us enormously, if we were introduced as Home Office liaison people, rather than the shadow men of the Intelligence Services – especially when we have to visit the provinces. It makes it so much harder for the people we interview to remember those important little details that can break a case when they're terrified of saying the wrong thing. Almost as soon as you've confessed your profession, they put up a wall, and you've got to charm them and smarm your way in, all over again.'

'Do you think this business in Whitborough and that human chain at Greenham Common yesterday is a tit for tat response to these expulsions? They must suspect by now we've got names and addresses from one of their pet Ivans.'

'It's certainly possible. But it's up to us to pin the tail on the donkey. Whether it's Russian or Irish, we'll get the bastards. There are only a few sympathisers in CND – and they're bottom of the pile people, unless our intelligence is defective. Personally, I'm not convinced there's a link. Can you imagine the KGB – midstream with those hairy lesbians at Greenham Common? They'd be petrified.'

Chapter Eleven

Sunday Lunch at the Shipley Browns'

At eleven o'clock on Sunday morning, Mary took the bus from Burniston to Whitborough, to have lunch with her parents and her brother. It was the only time they came together, apart from Christmas Day, since the day she had left home to pursue her obsessions. Mary grew to dread the gentle interrogation and teasing which accompanied her visits. But she knew there was no credible way of avoiding their Sunday ritual, if she wanted to avoid the possibility of losing her financial umbilical cord and with it any chance of maintaining her position in the commune. It was also the only time she could take phone calls in relative privacy, as the payphone in the Scout hut was fixed to the wall beside the kitchen door.

Within ten minutes of her arrival, the Shipley Brown family telephone rang and was picked up by Mary's brother Archie, even though he knew who the call must be for.

'Maaaaary… it's for you-hoo.'

'For me? Oh ta… thanks Arch. Yo, what's up?' said Mary, taking the phone gracefully from her brother.

'Mary? *Mike.* Listen – me and Digger can't mek it tonight.'

'MIIIKE!'

'Summat's come up at work. We've gotta go in later. The

boss wants us to finish the paint on the camper we're gutting, so it can cure in time for the new trim and decals on Tuesday. We'll have to stay past seven. It'll tek us an hour to get cleaned up after. We'll never mek it over in time.'

'I've been planning this for months! Who am I going to get to do this with now?'

'Look Shipley, don't burn my ears okay. I've gotta go in, y'know? Some of us have to bloody work for a living. I ain't got no trust fund money coming in like you. The job comes first. Why don't you ring Gaz – he's not doing owt until he starts at the Tech next term?'

'That's not fair…'

'It's true though, innit?'

'Don't be mean Mike.'

'*ME* be mean. *That's rich*… so, what about Gaz…'

'He's going to Leeds with Cassandra to see Discharge. I can't believe everybody's doing something else.'

'Well that ain't nobody's fault but yours is it? You should have given us a bit of notice. After what you said to Aisha I should be telling you to piss off anyway, actually. You can be a real dick sometimes Mary. How's the head by the way?'

'I've got a lump.'

'No shit.'

'Don't bring her back to the hut Mike – please.'

'I doubt she'd want to come back to see you Mary. Anyway… have you tried Ian? *He* might be free. Penny's not doing anything either, as far as I know.'

'Penny hates me.'

'Well Ian then…'

'Ian's too tall…'

'Too tall for what? You're going after dark anyway…
What's it matter?'

'I s'pose.'

'It's your call anyway. I've got to go. I'll see you later
okay… oh, and by the way, unless you want to be in a gang of
your own, it might be best not to bawl out your friends and
call us idiots – just a thought, dumbass.'

'Okay – yeah sorry. I'll ring him now.'

Ian Crouch, one of Whitborough's tallest underachievers,
splashed a cap full of Blue Bols on his chest, after his
shower, as a substitute for his empty reserve of Brut 33.
Then the payphone rang in the communal hallway of the
house he rented on Leather Lane with three students from
Whitborough Sixth Form College and Robin the Druid, a
mad-eyed acid casualty who walked around the town in
a dark brown velvet cloak and Jesus sandals. Ian got to the
phone just as Robin appeared at the top of the stairs.

'If it's Sauron, you ain't seen me – right brother?' hissed
Robin, whose only concession to modesty was a tatty brown
hand towel secured with a clothes peg. A tinfoil tulip, with a
burning roll-up inside its petals, hung from his forehead on a
huge blob of sticky gel.

'Uh huh – right Rob, we're sound buddy. Hello?'

'Ian, it's Mary. Don't hang up… I need your help for
Operation Donkey. Mike and Jim let me down.'

'I'm off for a game of pool in town.'

'Well now you can help me free some abused donkeys
instead; can you think of anything more important than that?
You can have a game of pool another night.'

'But…'

'What!'

'They were gonna let me try for the team tonight. Against the Jack of Both Sides.'

'So what's more important – their freedom, or your pool game? I can't believe I'm having to try and argue for them with you.'

'They'll still be there tomorrow won't they?'

'Are you really suggesting they put up with another cruel night in captivity, so you can try out for some damn pub's pool team?'

'How's it cruel? It's a brand new bloody stable. *It were built by a bloody donkey charity– and they're getting their grub free. I have to buy my own bloody food.*'

'I can't believe I'm hearing this... what about the cause!'

'Yeah... that's weekends. Weeknights I go to the pub.'

'It's Easter Sunday...'

'I'm doing summat.'

'Wouldn't it be tragic if Abbi found out about you and your problem? Your little mates...'

'What?'

'The ants in your pants.'

'You wouldn't Mary. You wouldn't dare.'

'Wouldn't I...*Ian.*'

'Don't Mary... I mean it. I'll...'

'Just help me out – and she'll never know you had crabs.'

'Don't even think about it Shipley – I mean it...'

'I'll pick you up at 8. Opposite Tito's lorry park on Higher Gunstone,' said Mary, as fast as she could get her words out, before hanging up.

76

The York to Whitborough train arrived at Whitborough Station at 12.38, bursting at the seams. Senior field agent James Stocke and his subordinate Bruce Dickson of MI5,who were travelling first class in their own compartment, waited for the train's corridor to clear before disembarking, observing the arrivals and departure gate and concourse from their seats for any suspicious-looking individuals or groups.

'Looks clear,' remarked Bruce.

'On time too. Right. Let's go and meet our host. He should be outside in a red Cortina estate. I think I'll have a shower and a change of clothes first of all. This train smells like all the ones in East Berlin.'

'What do they smell of?'

'Stale sausage– and fear.'

'Welcome to the GDR.'

'You can checkout any time you like…'

'But you can never leave…'

'It never dates, that song, though I'm a Scott Walker man myself. Are you an Eagles man Bruce?'

'I've got the album.'

'I seem to recall we relocated somebody from northeast Scotland to this place,' said Stocke, checking the next platform.

'Witness protection sir?'

'No. The other sort. Hobson's choice. A plus one.'

'What did they do?'

'Diplomatic incident. It's on file in the Cod War archives.'

'What's the clearance?'

'Highly Classified. Name of Crosbie. Nasty piece of work… Scottish Mafia.'

Barnett Crosbie, the host for Easter Monday's annual Battle of the Bands competition, was a man with a very singular reputation, and the manager of Mystery City, Whitborough's premier rock nightclub, owned by Manshipps Estates, one of the town's larger post-war real estate empires.

It was one of three clubs owned by the group within Whitborough, the closest to the heart of the old town and harbour, and some distance from its sister venues, Victoria's Penthouse and the Orange Tree, which catered for the conventional majority of holidaymakers and locals within the areas around the town centre. They also owned the only nightclub in Bridlington – the Cock and Hen Club – and the American Bars, a dance hall-cum-working men's club in Filey that featured a bar named after Frankie Laine; but Whitborough was the main focus of their operations.

Barnett's appointment as manager had been rubber-stamped in less time than was typical for such a position, due to the withdrawal of all but one of the candidates, from the second round of interviews. The previous incumbent, Bruce Butcher, had suddenly disappeared from his static caravan above Cayton Bay. Though this did not give Manshipps any real indication of the iniquitous narrative unfolding behind their backs. Bruce was very hard to locate at the best of times, habitually vague about his habits and liaisons.

Manshipps were duped because their primary focus had been to fill the gap in time for their new appointee to bed in before the summer season, which meant they were not as thorough and diligent as they would normally have been, establishing the validity of Barnett's references.

Once past the brief and reasonably satisfactory probation period – during which Barnett diligently applied himself to learning everything about their operation and the partners, their histories, strategies and ethos, meeting his co-workers, and familiarising himself with his responsibilities – Barnett began to treat the various streams of income the club generated as his own personal piggy bank.

By the time the repercussions of his appointment began to show up in their audits, it was too late for the partners and directors of Manshipps to act. The estate office staff, the bar staff and doormen who prospered in his care all knew of his embezzling, but Barnett was never confronted. Because Barnett was a gangster.

In the beginning, there had been nothing in his cast or bearing to alert Manshipps to his true character or predilections. They had been more concerned initially that he seemed to be a man on the brink of a stroke or some kind of seizure – slight in stature, with a recurring cough, limp mousey hair and a permanent sheen of sweat over a pallid, waxy complexion. He was no one's idea of a thug. But it was this false frailty, allied to his shocking mercurial violence and the bullet-studded truncheon his brother had made in metalwork classes at Dundee Technical College that had propelled him to the upper heights of Aberdeen's criminal underworld.

MI5 had put an early end to his ambitions north of the border, on the orders of the Foreign Office, when Barnett made history, by being the first private citizen of the United Kingdom to order the successful sinking of an Icelandic gunboat in the middle of negotiations at the end of the third and final Icelandic Cod War – his revenge for the treatment his nephew had endured after straying into their territory in his brother's trawler. He had been invited to 'retire' by the

Security Service to the seaside town of his choice across the border in England after his jail sentence; or suffer an accident of the kind in which there was no prospect of a happy outcome, or indeed any kind of outcome in which he would be walking and breathing.

So Barnett had come to Whitborough and applied himself to the task of accumulating enough of someone else's money for a comfortable retirement, targeting the cash registers of Manshipps Estates. He chose his prey carefully, appraising the character and histories of men he was to deprive, to ensure the reaction from his victims to his ambitions would not be anything more serious than the simmering resentment of men who discover they have been beaten at their own game, though as an insurance against any retaliatory actions, he compiled a dossier of their own less than legitimate activities; appending several newspaper clippings of his own, that were mailed out to the partners, with invitations to a private meeting, where they were witness to several selective episodes of his own frenzied violence.

There was at least a happy outcome for the office staff, who were delighted to take delivery of new desks, chairs, a suite, fax and copier after his outbursts.

For two years, he had never been challenged. There had even been a mild thaw in his icy relationship with the directors, which no one in the firm could ever have anticipated in the beginning. He continued to steal their money, though the amount he embezzled never altered, in terms of both the amount and the timing. It was to all intents and purposes, a direct debit for services rendered, though never invoiced.

What Manshipps received in kind, for the honour of employing a professional felon, was a smoothly-run nightclub without any incidents of violence. Since Barnett's arrival, there had been no bills for damages. No misbehaviour or sickness from the staff. And no predation from other criminal elements in Whitborough or sabotage from rivals. Barnett's presence had bestowed an invisible golden halo of protection over their oddball asset. The directors had grudgingly come to realise that Manshipps had more stability with him than without him.

He had originally been granted permission to leave Aberdeen with one companion, and chose James Stone, his often redundant protector and number two. In physical terms, he was a big brother figure to Barnett's sickly child. A small heavyset wardrobe of knotted muscle, gristle and malevolence with the presence of Charlton Heston's Moses. 'Begg Jamesy' fell upon the heads of those who had displeased his master, like the black shadow of a barn– and left those who had crossed him in much the same state of health as someone who had been crushed by one, but his apparent invincibility was really a sham, and his outbursts were little more than a quick and easy way to release the anxiety that came from the fear of being exposed as a former building site pervert.

Jamesy's dark secret was his unnatural love of PVA, a passion that had first manifested itself during his CITB Bricklaying apprenticeship. In the trade it was used as an admixture for cement; though for Stone, it had become the focus of new and bizarre compulsions, which acted as a safety valve from his violent rages.

One of his less alarming rituals involved smearing a thick layer over his hands and forearms to his elbows; drying out the film of glue under a hand dryer, then locking himself in the end toilet cubicle for the sensory orgasm that came upon him during the peel-off. Because of this, his forearms were hairless and he smelled like a primary school woodwork tools cupboard. But it relaxed him sufficiently to keep his ferocious temper at bay, and got him through the day without him resorting to expressing himself with his fists.

All of this was blown apart when he was discovered by a cleaner at the moment of orgasm and asked to relinquish his place on the course. Through desperation he had gone to work in a bar, eventually meeting Barnett over the unconscious bodies of two Rangers' fans he had put to sleep with his forehead.

James was often teased for his lack of social skills and unblinking seriousness, but never more than once.

Inside the transformed former sailcloth and rigging factory that was Mystery City, there had been no altercations or even so much as a cross word, since Barnett's coronation.

The shocking details of his first tantrum on the door travelled swiftly up the grapevine throughout the town, cementing his status as the foremost psychopath of his generation. The carcasses of the two splintered exit doors and their mutilated panes of safety glass – with two head-shaped depressions – were left propped outside over the weekend, as a warning totem to any rivals who might wish to examine his technique.

Mystery City had two rock nights on Friday and Saturday. An 'alternative' night on Thursday, a student night on Wednesday and a classic film night on Monday. Or, if the projector was being repaired – a comedian. Barnett lived in a self-contained flat within the loft space and commissioned a suspended office and viewing platform beneath inside the old lift cage frames, from where he could survey the bars and dance floors below,while Jimmy sometimes bedded down on a cot in the projector and utilities room if he had drunk too much to walk home, where he could be alone, with his glue.

On Bank Holiday Sunday, Barnett was compelled to spend a dreary afternoon and the longest part of the evening watching the construction of a large stage inside his club by technicians from Whitborough Technical College and the local Musicians' Union, for the annual Battle of the Bands competition the following night. A very dull but necessary duty, for which he had prepared by opening the bar, helping himself to a bottle of Bells, a copy of the *Racing Post* and the Sunday edition of *The Scotsman*, knowing nothing about the live music scene, apart from the control and intimidation of crowds and the exact amount of violence required to stamp out any dissent. He didn't want to engage the stage builders, the electricians or the technicians and turned his back on the whole proceedings while Jamesy scuttled from group to group, looking over the shoulders of the workmen with a face that mixed fascination and suspicion with envy and awe.

Chapter Twelve

Jailbreak

The anarchy car was a white Ford Escort Mk1 estate called Chris, after Yul Brynner's character in *The Magnificent Seven*, whom Mary had worshipped from afar since her last year at primary. Though Mary's car smoked a lot less than her movie star cowboy, its lower bodywork reflected his black-clad limbs, now its sills and wheel arches were daubed with blackboard paint and Hammerite, to slow the progress of decay, which had already begun to creep into its bones some years before. But Mary loved him and washed him religiously in Turtle Wax; though his springs were tired, his paintwork shone like the white walls of an operating theatre. If it hadn't been for the BOLLOCKS to CAPITALISM sticker on the back window, the old Escort could easily have been mistaken for the cherished transport of an English clergyman.

Mary and Chris arrived to collect Ian in front of Tito's Goods Vehicles forecourt at 8pm, with the front passenger seat as far back as it would go, so her accomplice could arrange his limbs in relative safety. Mary drew up, put Chris in neutral and opened the passenger door.

'What's with all the bloody straps and collars – are you going to an S&M party on the way back..?' remarked Ian, looking at the pile of horse tack on her back seat as he tried to squeeze himself in.

'They're bridles Ian…'

'I see you've come dressed for it,' he scoffed, still trying to needle his chauffeur.

'What do you mean?'

'If someone points a torch at you tonight you'll stand out like a bloody Christmas tree; haven't you got any camos?'

'I've got my greatcoat… what's wrong with it?' said Mary, defensively.

'It's got six king-size, shiny buttons on the front. With them an' yer earrings you'll look like a friggin' chandelier if you get lit up, you daft cow.'

'Don't you call *me* a daft cow!'

'I'll call you what I like, because you're blackmailing me. Aren't you Shipley? I'm only here, instead of in a nice warm pub, because you're threatening to tell my bird I had to go to the friggin' clap clinic– so don't get bloody smart with me.'

'Well what am I supposed to do *Ian*? There's no one else. I'm desperate…'

'So you thought you'd just blackmail me did you? *Because there's no one else,*' he sneered, 'you're mad.'

'It's not mad! Just belt up and stop complaining.'

The much-loved herd of donkeys that had walked the sands of Victoria Bay since the 1920's, giving rides to generations of little boys and girls, were stabled in their own purpose-built paddock in a steep field, on the lower slopes of Oliver's Mount, and enjoyed spectacular views across to the wolds, over the Mere and Higher Gunstone, the secondary arterial route into Whitborough – along Ogmundarson Dyke.

Their paddock was reached by a single dirt track road through woodland, on a fork adjoining Queen Mary's Rd, which linked Higher and Lower Gunstone, three quarters of a mile from the sands of Victoria Bay. Once the herd had returned to their quarters and were secure inside the stable block, they were alone for the night. The perimeter was secured by a galvanised grid fence and steel gate that was padlocked at night. Only the rear of the compound, which opened onto a steep field, was unfenced, though a dense hedge around its borders meant no other man-made barrier in front, or beyond, was necessary.

Mary's plan for releasing the herd involved approaching the compound from a higher field, below Mountside Hairpin. She hoped she would be able to pick the stable door lock, once they were on the yard, and then lead the animals through another gate at the top of the field and into the woods to freedom, thus avoiding the CCTV cameras covering the main gate. Mary and Ian parked in a lay-by beside the racetrack at Woodland Leap, sat in silence and waited for the sun to sink below Jacobs Mount.

Forty-five minutes later, the two kidnappers reached the edge of the donkey paddock and knelt down in the weeds and grass at the edge of the yard, checking the windows for lights or signs of activity, though the compound was quiet and nothing stirred within. Mary got to her feet and stepped forward impulsively, cracking a large dry twig.

'Shush…'

'Shush me!'

'Stop making so much bloody noise then! There might still be somebody about, Mary.'

'There's never anyone around here after seven, anyway, they don't scare me…'

'You haven't seen the bigger one. She's built like Les Dawson. I seen her on Vicky Bay hauling kids on an' off their backs like they wuz packets of crisps.'

'There aren't any lights on. Let's get a bit closer.'

The two commandos paused.

'Hold my bridles.'

'Just a minute. Just wait a minute.'

'Why?'

'Quiet. Just listen.'

'We're wasting time Ian.'

'I'm making sure there's no one about. D'you wanna get arrested or duffed up?'

'There's nobody here, I told you.'

Mary and Ian reached the steps before the door to the stables, listening for a few seconds before attempting to pick the lock.

'Turn around Ian.'

'What?'

'Turn around and watch the yard.'

'Why?'

'Because I don't like it when people watch me doing stuff, okay... watch the trees or something.'

Ian huffed and turned around. 'I don't believe I'm doing this. It's not even sane.'

Mary opened her purse and took out a set of lock picks. After a couple of minutes, she had sprung the latch and opened the door.

'How d'you learn to do that Shipley?'

'My dad's gardener showed me when I was a girl.'

'Cool. Can you show me?'

'No, Ian. Right...let's do it,' said Mary a little nervously, feeling for the light switch.

'Bugger me – this is smart,' gasped Ian, as the lights came on inside the stables.

'Just remember, it's a prison.'

'Nice though…'

'Ian, it doesn't matter how… how…'

'What? How nice it looks?'

'I wasn't going to say that.'

'It is though 'int it. If I were a donkey, I'd be dead chuffed holed up in here.'

'That's not the point – they're prisoners. They have no freedoms.'

'But they're all pretty healthy-lookin'. Are you sure we should be doing this? What if they end up wandering on the road and causing an accident?'

'They can go where they want when they're free.'

'They can't though can they. We're right next to a main road leading onto Gunstone; what if they get hit by a bloomin' car?'

'We're not releasing them in town.'

'Where then?'

'We take them down onto the beach then walk up the coast.'

'Have you checked the tides?'

'You're just being negative. Who cares! Petty details like that – they'll be free. That's what you should be thinking – we're doing our bit for the cause. Freedom for animals… freedom from cruelty, from vivisection.'

'Oh come on… they're not exactly mistreated or starved are they? Or vivisected.'

Mary snorted derisively. 'There's bigger issues.'

'Bigger issues! Like what?'

'Animal exploitation. They're being exploited. Every day, they're exploited.'

'So am I. I'm exploited – but no one wants to kidnap me and dump me in the bloody countryside, miles from anywhere without any food. I've done one frigging sponsored walk – and that was enough.'

'They can eat grass Ian.'

'How's that better than oats? And how are you gonna move 'em anyway?'

'We walk them.'

'Are they gonna go with us though? They're a bit stubborn aren't they – mules 'n' donkeys..?'

'Of course they will, they'll go wherever we take them.'

'Cuz we're vegetarians?' Mary gave him a look. 'Your show Mary,' said Ian, giving in, 'hope you know what you're doing. This one's called Pepper,' he said, reading the name plate on the stall, 'cool name.'

'Don't just stand around Ian, they need bridles on.'

'I don't know how, *do I*… I play pool. I'm not a friggin' rustler.'

'Come over and watch me then,' moaned Mary, unfolding her carefully tied bridles and reins. 'Open the door.'

'It's not gonna run out is it?' he said, covering the bolt on the door with his hand.

'They're not like horses Ian, look at them – they're so docile and trusting,' she cooed.

'Well all right, are you ready then?' said Ian warily. He lifted the latch and drew the door towards them, but Pepper remained standing in his stall. Mary approached him with the bridle, though the donkey never flinched, despite the stink of her dreadlocks.

'See? Easy,' she said, pleased as punch after a minute of fiddling, kissing Pepper's nose affectionately. 'Now you have a go with one of the others.'

'All right, I'll give it a shot, so howd' you learn how to do that?'

'I had two horses and a Shetland pony – for Ryedale's gymkhana – well, I say that, but I had to sh… why are you looking at me like that?' complained Mary suddenly, looking at Ian's overdone expression of surprise.

'You had two horses *and* a pony?'

'So..?'

'Yeah – you just said you had two horses *and* a pony Mary.'

'So– what about it?' she fumed, suddenly losing her temper. 'Just get the bridles on the rest of them for God's sake and stop asking me stupid questions!'

'Don't talk to me like that Mary – or I'll walk.'

'All right, all right… just… be quick will you…'

Mary had clammed up a little, realising she had let slip a less than complimentary detail from her previous life as a well-kept public schoolgirl.

Sweetie, the most stubborn and headstrong animal in the stable, kicked the wall of her stall with her back hoof to express her displeasure at being disturbed after hours, as Mary led Pepper and Ginny to a tethering pole beside the door to the ramp and the exit onto their field. Then she went back to 'rescue' the other animals and check Ian had properly fastened their bridles.

A Séance

At the Valhalla Retirement Home,
(900 yards from the stables).

The Gold Cup lounge on the south face of Whitborough's infamous Valhalla Retirement Home, overlooked a narrow flagstone patio and a well-kept lawn, which fell away from the house on a gentle gradient to the boundary – ringed by a four-course sandstone block wall and inner hedge where the last stretch of Lower Gunstone met the top of Ramsgill High Street.

The extension borrowed much from the layout, dimensions and feel of a typical motorcycle showroom to which the proprietors had added the fixtures, fittings and furniture of a Tsarist ballroom. It was freezing cold in winter – stifling in summer – and preposterously ostentatious all year round, and the most popular communal space in the building, with its peerless views of the best summer traffic jams, and the umbrella-wrecking winter gales and storms, that only the North Sea's storm triangle coast was capable of producing.

It was also the venue for Elsie Cakebread's Sunday night séances – a weekly treat for her residents and guests, when the sun had slipped below Jacobs Mount and the heavy gold brocade curtains were drawn across its great glass panes, blocking out the curious stares of passing motorists, nosy pedestrians and gawping taxi drivers. Valhalla was something of a rarity within the world of old people's homes. And never had an empty bed.

Instead of the usual room numbers that were so common to the other establishments around it, each room in the Cakebread household took its name from the great lists and rolls of motor racing history, or notorious incidents, and characters from the rock and roll halls of fame and infamy. Valhalla catered for the type of elderly ladies and gentlemen who had enjoyed the kind of lifestyle that went with loud music, fast bikes and beer, and did not want to spend their last few years deposited in front of a television between meals, ignored by a group of uninterested teenagers masquerading as care assistants, who, in comparison with the residents, had barely left the scrotum. If you were in Valhalla, you were never likely to be bored.

Behind the polished aluminium front doors of its Art Deco facade, which mirrored the entrance and exits of the town's biggest cinema, lay the Bray Hill foyer, named after the terrifying downhill straight from the Isle of Man TT races.

In the right-hand corner of the foyer, behind a shimmering silver cylinder, stood the Nurburgring staircase, a structure straight from the imagination of M.C. Escher. For those reluctant to sample its bizarre curves, a Stannah stairlift and a more conventional flight of steps – the Staircase to Heaven – on the left, offered the safest and most direct route to the first-floor bedrooms, especially after one or two of Elsie's speciality calvados and rum cocktails.

Each room in Valhalla featured a spacious en suite, an

intercom system and a dumb waiter (a small elevator for food, packages and luggage). The residents also had the option to use the Jim Morrison memorial bath house and sauna on the ground floor –between Hell's Kitchen and Death Disco.

On the first floor there were twenty single private rooms, on two wings to the left and right of a library and cinema, and the MotorFloyd sensory lounge inbetween.

On the second floor there were ten more rooms, a video games suite and a flight simulator room, housing Sopwith Camel, Spitfire and Harrier flight simulators. With enough fifty pence pieces, one could dispatch two generations of Germans or a token Argentinian in an exported French plane, subject to your own skill and élan, whilst the attic, reached by means of a winding iron staircase, housed the Frank-N-Furter observatory and Gothic Planetarium.

Valhalla's landscaped grounds occupied a rectangular plot, set into the lower slopes of Oliver's Mount over three ascending terraces.

The first level was set out as a patio and barbecue area, with benches, cane recliners and a handful of small garden reading rooms. A fire pit, model village and scale models of Stonehenge and Glastonbury Tor occupied the second.

On the uppermost terrace, a U-shaped clubhouse, pool and snooker room enclosed the firing platform on the shooting range, which was accessed through patio doors on the bridging corridor between the wings.

The target wall on the range, which was faced with galvanised wire cages filled with hardcore, was also blessed by a third layer of protection, in the form of the stout sectional concrete barriers– beloved of British Rail, that ensured anything living which dared to cross the embankment below the railway line beyond, survived intact, the odd wild shot from the residents sometimes fell upon the tracks of the Whitborough to York train. But the noise of the diesel engines accelerating usually masked the clatter of shotgun pellets bouncing off the carriage roofs.

It was Elsie's first circle, since the sinking of HMS *Brazen* and the brawl the local paper had sensationally titled 'the Milk Race Massacre' the week before. They had two other guests from the Spiritualist Church on Meddon Street and an anonymous member of the Black Hand Coven, Isla Binnie, wife of Tony Binnie, the first victim of Lindsay Boldwood, the county's new werewolf.

Isla was masquerading as a guest of the Spiritualists with a cover story that pretended to portray her as a wronged wife, who was still unsure whether her husband had run away from his debts, or moved into the next world by accident or suicide.

Elsie had arranged her sitters in their usual circular pattern, instructing the group to join hands after performing her ritual of protection and asking the group to let their thoughts clear. She now directed their eyes to the flame above the single pillar candle, in the centre of the table, their only permitted light source for the duration.

Elsie dipped her chin towards her bosom and closed her eyes, squeezing the hands placed benignly in hers, as she attempted to connect with the spirits on the lower plains of the astral world.

'Is there anybody there?' she asked softly, taking a long breath, though her words barely had time to settle in the air before two commemorative Isle of Man TT plates leapt off their hooks on the wall, into a scrum of cushions covering the back of an expensively-upholstered armchair.

A haunting black and white photo print of Alice Cooper, mounted in a clip frame, followed motorcycle legends Mike Hailwood and Giacomo Agostini, flung from the picture rail by invisible forces into a bunch of ripening bananas, as the table began to rattle, drilling its legs manically on the parquet floors, before taking to the air like an overloaded Sea King helicopter. Then the table suddenly clattered back down to terra firma, shuddering like an epileptic piledriver, before rising up yet again at a tilt by its right legs.

'Lean left! Left!' yelled Alan Backhouse, another sensitive and a former sidecar racer, who knew all there was to know about leaning into the kerbs of certain death. The table connected with the tiled floor once more, only to rise again by incremental millimetres, shaking and rattling its screws as it rocked and buzzed.

Elsie's precious reproduction Faberge eggs began dancing a jig on their mounts, keeping rhythm with the bone-shaking clatter of the table's legs. But the vibrations of the spirits were becoming so unbearable, they were threatening to crack the huge glass panes in the windows behind the living room.

'Always knew how to crash, old Croxford,' said Mark Lockhart, under his breath, catching sight of two more racing veterans, immortalised in china, falling to earth.

The table took to the air once more, and began to oscillate more wildly. Elsie's party were only seconds away from running for the safety of the foyer when the vibrations abruptly ceased and the table crashed to the floor. A wind which wasn't a wind, but the sound of rushing ectoplasm collecting and carrying disembodied voices now came to the fore… then Elsie tipped forward in her stupor and began to vocalise, though one of her guests almost drowned her out.

'ARGHHHHHH! YA C★★★S!' yelled Isla Binnie, as one of the table legs split her toenail.

'MURDERED-ME!' cried a heavily accented male voice, from the throat of their host.'

'That's the bleedin'mayor!' said Gareth Tonks, nearly breaking hands with a gurn of disgust, name-checking their seafood-loving former first citizen of the borough. 'The fat turd.'

A gelatinous white lump shot from Elsie's mouth and landed in the centre of the table with a wet slap, quivering on the gold satin embroidery of the regal antimacassar she used as a table runner. Several of the guests heaved, holding their hands over their mouths. Isla, already hovering on the edge of nausea, from the pain in her toe, threw up in her neighbour's lap.

'AWWWW! NOOOOO! You dirty bitch!' cried one of her escorts, losing all her spiritual sisterliness.

'What the f★★k is that *thing* on the f★★king table?' cried Mr Tonks, screwing up his face.

'It looks like a scallop…'

Isla threw up again. Over her own portion of the table…

'GET THAT F★★KING HISTORY TEACHER!' yelled the spirit of the recently deceased Mayor, firing another gelatinous bullet of shellfish from the spirit realm, past Elsie's burgundy lips.

'Gate back tae hell, yer pot-bellied preck,' moaned Isla, clutching her foot, wiping something that looked like Pot Noodle from her chin with one of Elsie's brocade placemats.

'IN ST MARY'S!' cried the voice, which was suddenly replaced by the bullying shout of another male spirit voice.

'OOT MA WAY, YA MUSSEL-GUZZLEN BASTARD…'

'ANTHONY – EZ THAT YEW?' called Isla desperately, still clutching her blackening toe which was throbbing so hard, she thought it might burst.

'ETTS ME ISLA, AHM FIGHTEN FAE SPACE HERE HEN!… C★★T!'

'Are ya dayd Anthony? JEESHUSH! Ma fecken toe hutts!'

'AYE, I'D SAY SO, RIGHT 'ANUFF. MA HEED'S COMPOSTENN ENN THE WOODS. AN' THE REST GORT EAT'N. BY A FECKEN WOLF – BACK OFF! YA PRECK! shouted the ghost of Tony Binnie, at another competing spirit, who was trying to break his hold on Elsie's faculties.'

'A wolf? Are yee right enn the hayd? 'Who's thaa ya fightenn?'

'MA HEEDS ENN THE WOODS WOMAN! AHM DAYD FAY NUTHEN! FAY NUTHEN! WHAT THE HELL'S THART SHTUFF ORN YER CHENN?'

'There's nuthen orn ma chenn,' replied his wife without much conviction before she recovered her dignity, 'dedd yee find the gold?'

'GOLD?.. What gold?'said Alan, suddenly alert.

'Shut yer fecken ears– youze. Ahm talken tae ma fecken hushzband.'

'How do you know it's him..?'

'Pess off. Ahh know mah Anthony. Steck ya friggen fengers in y'fecken ears. Ahv no gev yoo permeshen tae hear wa' conversation.'

'YER DREFTENN HEN! AH CANNAE HOLD ON

HERE... THEY'RE PULLEN ME BACK. HE ATE MA
PAGER! THE WOLF!'

'Yer pager – yer kedden?'

'AHM NO KEDDEN! THE LANDLAIRD O' THE
SHI... THE SHHHIRE...'

Suddenly, the door to the foyer flew open and a howling
wind blew out the candle, plunging the table into darkness
and agitating the folds of the heavy curtains. A tall, stocky
figure stood in silhouette in front of the hall lights beyond.

'Does anyone know how to change the Guinness ovver
Else? We're dying o' bloody thirst out 'ere.'

Derek Beautimann and Maureen Moment, the Grand Wizard
and Deputy of the Black Hand Coven, sat close together on
separate armchairs in a quiet corner of the Royal Hotel's
lounge bar, talking quietly, amongst themselves. They had
met to discuss what to do with their share of half a fortune
in gold and jewels which Derek had located and excavated
several days before. Though no one who knew their true
circumstances would describe them as blessed, one of them
was at least hopeful of a better future, once the matter of a
certain curse was neutralised. Unfortunately, it did not look
as though their fraternity of wizards and witches would
survive the spring, but the manner of the coven's dissolution
had to be faced.

'I've come to a decision Maureen,' announced her
accomplice and employer. 'I'm going to resign as Grand
Wizard and Master of Ceremonies. I've no desire to continue
to entertain a troop of fools and delinquents. From now on,
they can be the masters of their own destinies. I shall say they
have my best wishes for the future, be magnanimous and

gracious, but I'm afraid I've come to a crossroads with our society.'

'I wouldn't have put it quite like that Derek. Nobody expects you to "entertain" them. What on earth will they do if you go?'

'They'll have the pleasure of arguing amongst themselves I expect. Why should you care what happens to them?'

'Why do you have to be so rude about them? They're not bad people. Most of them look up to you, if only you'd bother to notice.'

'Oh they're polite enough on their own, granted. I've no wish to go on record as having made a blanket character assassination of my own coven. But when they're all together, it's a different story isn't it? They're impossible… I'm sorry, but they'll just have to manage themselves from now on and that's my final decision.'

'Well, there's nothing more to be said then. Are you going to do it in writing?'

'Maureen – would you like to think about what you just said?'

'No – why?'

'May I suggest that you do?'

'No – you can't.'

'Well… I'll just implicate myself in my own hand shall I? And end up on the front page of the *News of the World*, with my head superimposed on top of a pantomime wizard's cape – and a goat tucked under my arm. That'll do wonders for my career in the law.'

'Oh…I hadn't thought about it that way.'

'I think it's best if I do the thinking. That's the way it is at work, and that's the way it's going to stay outside.'

'Are you giving it up then? The dark side…'

'Not exactly… I'm going to see if I can find some kind of parallel satisfaction in golf. There must be some kind of supernatural force involved in putting a tiny ball into a tiny hole, with something that looks like a joke shop drain rod. Trevor and James are always arguing about their damned golf handicaps, so I've decided to take them up on their invitation to accompany them as an associate member and see if it stirs anything in me. I just hope they've got some other avenues of conversation. There's no bigger bore than an over-keen amateur sportsman, except those poor unfortunates who think soap operas are the highest form of entertainment.'

'Poor unfortunates? Am I a poor unfortunate? Sometimes, you can be a really nasty piece of work, do you know that? Let me tell you something, Derek Beautimann; *Coronation Street* is the best social drama on television. It's real life, with real people, with real problems – well, hypothetical real people – it's not cheap telly, like you seem to think it is. They've won awards… almost every year since the 1960s. People don't like having their tastes criticised – I don't criticise your tastes do I?'

'But don't you find it bland?'

'Certainly not!'

'Well… don't you get enough *real life– in* real life?'

'You go to the theatre don't you? It's the same thing…'

'Television and theatre are very different mediums Maureen. And vastly different experiences. A play is a cleverly condensed construct, story – an experience told by the skill and dedication of actors in the midst of live performance, without the smothering dominance of huge production sets. At the end of a play, there is always a resolution, *an outcome*.

A message. Soap operas drag on for decades... there's no... no nourishment for the spirit. They're monotonous and mundane to the point of... tedium.'

'Have you ever been punched by a woman Derek? Because you're getting very close.'

On the middle slopes of Oliver's Mount, the BADCOW kidnap and rescue mission's progress had stalled. Ian had parked his two donkeys, Sweetie and Pepper, beside the boundary hedge and gone forward to a break in the foliage at a stile, to try and find the source of some shouts and the noise of running boots beyond the hedge. He craned over the top plank and checked the road, which was swarming with teenage boys, wearing berets and camouflage jackets, grappling, shoving and wrestling each other. Two of the younger boys, at the edge off the melee, managed to break off and sprinted towards the stile, stumbling over the steps, panting like cross-country runners. They stopped momentarily and hesitated, looked at Ian for a second, then carried on running on the other side of the hedge, along the track towards the woods provisionally chosen by Mary for Operation Donkey.

Mary reached the stile just as the gang fight spilled over into the higher fields on the opposite side of the road, though there were at least two pairs of teenagers still wrestling on the verges in the gloom.

'I can't get the others to move, Ian. Something's spooked them – what's all that noise behind the hedge?' she asked, sounding unusually calm and reasonable.'

'The f**king Air Cadets are having a scrap; that's what's happening. A bloody night exercise.' I didn't think your luck was that bad Shipley, but you've picked a right pearler you have. Still, it's not all bad. The two little shits who ran past me dropped a four-pack of Watneys Pale Ale in the nettles,' he smirked, brandishing an open can. 'We're gonna have to take your nags back,' said Ian.'There's probably about forty of the bastards tear-arsing around, kicking the living shit out of each other and they'll all be getting picked up by their instructors in an hour. You're stuffed…'

'I'm not taking them back – not now.'

'Mary, the whole of this side of Oliver's Mount is full of crazy, belligerent little nut-job bastards – well only some of 'em are little. One of me brothers is in 739 Squadron; they might only be teenagers but they drink and fight like bloody maniacs. We'll have to go back.'

'Stay here with these two, Ian. I'll take the others back and we'll go with Pepper and Sweetie.'

'Mary… I'm telling you we can't do this tonight… we'll get spotted.'

'Pull your hood up then. *We go Ian*. Wait here – I'll be ten minutes.'

Chapter Thirteen

Bark at the Moon

Outside the door to Lindsay Boldwood's rooms in the Shirestones, a small crowd had gathered. Two middle-aged Scottish ladies, in Hawaiian-style costumes, were trying to explain to Gemma and Bonnie Naylor– Lindsay's holiday girls, what they had heard inside his rooms.

'I hudd shomeone banging the furniture lassie. Theyn there wuz thess tayrabble groan. Och, ett sooounded like shomeone was having a fett. I thenk yer boss musht bee havenn a wee bushtup… it's no nice tae heeeer. Wheyn yer jusht neyxt dooer, y'ken?'

'Aye – thurr's shome kind o' ar-namal enn there. It did'nae sooound too weyll.'

'*Mr Boldwood*? It's Gemma, Mr Boldwood…Are you all right in there?'

'*GROWWL.*'

'Bonnie – go and get the boys. Tell them there's a dog loose in Mr Boldwood's rooms.'

'How'd it get in there? We're on the second floor.'

'Maybe it's Mr Cunncliffe's Yorkie. When you see the boys, ask them to bring me his keys up.'

'That's never a Yorkie Gemma – get real…'

'Well it needs to come out… it can't stay in there and I'm not touching it. It smells of old wee.'

'GROWWWWL.'

'Are you sure we should open the door– what if it leaps out and bites someone? Lindsay might have locked it in there on purpose.'

'It doesn't sound like a Yorkie does it? Should we ring the police?'

'They'll jusht tell ye tae reng the dog warden peytull. Yon ar-namal's gort a nasty growl eh?'

'I'll get Dale and Matthew,' said Bonnie, striding off for the stairs. 'They can deal with it.'

'MR BOLDWOOD! ARE YOU THERE?'

'GRRRRRRR…'

'Och dear, ah thenk ye might need tae get ett orn a hayd collar.'

'My name's Gemma, Mrs Jensen.'

'Och aye… I see yurr name tag now. Weyll, I see you've gort thengs enn order. I'll take maself off doonstairs.'

Bonnie returned a few minutes later. 'The lads are just getting Thomas to watch the bar, Gem.'

'Lindsay's still not answering. He must be somewhere else.'

'He said he was coming up here for a bath. About fifteen minutes ago.'

'Well he's not in there now.'

'Maybe that thing in there, is the thing that Ian saw in the cellar – from the zoo,' said Bonnie. 'The same thing that ate all the mince and broke the door to the scullery.'

The Bingley Beach Boys were the most accomplished and coveted Beach Boys tribute band in the British Isles. It had taken Boldwood nearly two years of consistent pleading, bribery and flattery to persuade them to play an early Easter

Sunday set before their main gig at the Paul Murray Concert Hall in Whitborough later that same evening. They were certainly a big draw for his guests, and the crowning glory of the weekend's entertainment.

Thomas Hibbard, Boldwood's full-time chef had come out of the food prep area to watch the band and watch over the bar while Dale and Matthew went up to Boldwood's rooms to see what the girls were complaining about.

'What's up?' asked Matthew finally. When they reached the two sisters on the second landing, the girls were squatting down in front of Boldwood's key hole.

'My God… it's HUGE!'

'What is?'

'The thing in there – I can't tell…'

'Let me see Bonnie…'

'You can't spy on the boss like that Bonnie!' said Matthew sharply. 'Why'd you call us up here anyway?'

'What did you bring that surfboard all the way up here for?' asked Gemma, frowning.

'I don't want anybody clowning around with it downstairs – *that's why,'* replied Matthew indignantly. 'What's going on?'

'There's a dog in Lindsay's apartment, it's been growling at us.'

'It's not a dog,' said Bonnie.'I don't know what it is, but it's not a dog – it's enormous…'

'How did it get up here anyway?' said Dale.'

'How should we know?'

'All right – I'm only asking. Didn't Lindsay just come up here? You shouldn't be peering through his keyhole like some kind of perv.'

'Don't call me a perv – we've called him and knocked three times but he's not answering the door.'

'Well maybe he's not in there anymore – has anyone checked downstairs?'

'He's not in the hotel Matthew.'

'Why do you want to open the door anyway?'

'Two of the older ladies said they heard someone banging against the furniture and groaning. He could have passed out or something. If he's in there at all.'

'Or maybe that thing in there attacked him…'

'*GROWWWWL.*'

'Blimey – that dunt sound friendly…' said Matthew, as the two girls flashed him their best *told you so* expressions.'

'Let me have a peek', said Dale, bending down to the keyhole.

'What is it… can you see it?' asked Matthew.

'Nuthin'… can't see owt.'

'You must be able to see something!' snapped Gemma. 'Didn't you just hear it?'

'Gemma – don't be an arse,' replied Matthew.

'Still nothing,' mumbled Dale, standing up to rub his knees. 'You have a look Matt.'

'Ta,' said Matthew, taking his place by the door handle. The old keyhole on Boldwood's door was almost five times as high, and over three as wide as the aperture in a modern lock plate. Designed for the much larger keys from the early Victorian period, it was a veritable wind tunnel compared to what was now considered the norm. It was the frame into which the glaring yellow eyeball of their employer now rose and shone with malignant luminosity, locking onto the left eye of Master Matthew Parker.

'HOLY SHIT!'

Matthew fell backwards onto the carpet, just as the werewolf's front paws slammed through the one-inch gap at the bottom of the old door, tearing the suede on the front of Bonnie's shoe. Boldwood roared with anger, turning their blood to ice and began to tear out the carpet in front of the gripper below his door with his razor-sharp claws.

Even the Bingley Beach Boys, who were gliding down through the last few bars of 'When I Grow Up (To Be a Man)', heard the blood-curdling howl, but carried on regardless, like the professional musicians they were, subtly eyeballing each other.

The band's leader and guitarist Bert Chadwick, 'Chad' to his band mates, decided to gloss over the noise upstairs by cutting out the last few chords and waved his hand to lead the band into the sunlit uplands of 'Fun, Fun, Fun.'

Gemma screamed, Bonnie jumped back, Dale fled and Matthew slammed the nose of his surfboard onto the carpet gripper at the bottom of Boldwood's door, breaking off one of Boldwood's claws. The werewolf roared again and slammed its considerable bulk against the old door, to little effect. Then Matthew withdrew from the second landing once he saw the two sisters disappear down the staircase.

Dale ran to the payphone once they had reached the foyer and dialled 999.

'Hello?' said Dale, trying to steady his voice as his hands started to shake.

'Operator – which service do you require?'

'Ar-armed police… or the dog section?' said Dale. 'B-both I think.'

'I'm afraid I can only connect you to the nearest police

station, sir. They'll assess your request and offer you the appropriate service. Can I have your name and address and a short summary of your circumstances?'

'Dale Penny – The Shirestones Hotel in Cloughton. We've got a massive wolf in one of the bedrooms and the hotel's full of Scots. We've got a band on too…'

'Are you wanting the police for the dog, the Scots or the band sir?'

'IT'S NOT A DOG – IT'S A WOLF!'

'Please keep calm Mr Penny.'

'I'm sorry, but it really is a wolf.'

'Hold the line sir… I'm connecting you to Whitborough Police now.'

Boldwood jumped through the large glass pane of his bathroom window and crashed onto the decking below.

'What was that Matt?' asked Dale, while he waited to be connected to the police station by the operator. Matthew saw the retreating form of the werewolf through the half-panel door at the end of the through corridor and shut the door in the foyer as quietly as he could, ducking down under the bottom section to conceal himself.

'You're leaving girls,' said Matthew. 'When I've spoken to the cops, ring yer Dad and get 'im down here to pick you up. Me an' Dale will stick around with Thomas until the police get here then we'll go too.'

'Is it in the yard now?' asked Gemma nervously. 'Cos if it is we're staying in here. I think we should all go into the main lounge and close all the doors and shutters until the police arrive.'

'What about Lindsay? We can't just run out on him and Thomas… and the guests…'

Boldwood was ready to retrace his route to Kettleness and would be long gone before the police car arrived. It would be his most bloodthirsty night yet above Whitby and provoke a council of war amongst the farming community. But first, he had some unfinished business in Crescent Moon Kebabs on Pilger Street.

Chapter Fourteen

MI5 Safe House, Leeds LS2, Sunday Evening

When Colin Crawford eventually regained consciousness, there was no doubt in his mind that he was now in very serious trouble. Restrained and gagged inside a featureless, windowless room in complete darkness – at least it was very dark, at the margins of his vision, because his head and shoulders were trapped in the glare of intense white light. His hands had been shackled and chained to the thick steel tubing of the ambulance-style trolley he was laid upon. And his feet were secured in a similar manner to the same rail which ran around the bottom of the trolley outside the plastic-coated mattress. A wide leather restraining belt ran over his thighs above his knees. He was vaguely aware of a man standing behind his right shoulder. There was a plain wooden table to his front covering his thighs and lower limbs, which ached and throbbed with the same uncomfortable tightness as the pain in his forehead. Beyond the light, on the other side of the empty table, sat another man, languidly smoking a cigarette, his outline and features hidden in the shadows behind the bleaching brightness of the lights blinding his vision.

He had no idea how much time had passed since his loss of consciousness, caused by his self-inflicted injury, though it was beginning to dawn on him that he was now in the custody of people who were operating outside the law and the customs of his country and outside the rules of normal behaviour, so he decided to remain polite to avoid antagonising his captors. Somebody behind him began to unbuckle the bridle holding the leather block between his teeth.

'Name!'

'C…Crawford. Colin. I'm a jour…'

'Are you a spy Mr Crawford?'

'NO! No, I'm just a journalist. Can I have some water?'

'That is your *occupation*,' said the voice, disdainfully, 'this is not of any interest to us Mr Crawford.'

'Have you ever passed sensitive, confidential or secret information to representatives of a foreign power, for money or ideological reasons?' Crawford suddenly realised he must be in the hands of the Security Service, which was an improvement on the alternative. But he realised he was still in a world of trouble. He was going to have to tread very carefully.

'No, never. Can I have a drink please?'

'Give him some water,' said his interrogator, to the man behind him. 'You are a member of the Communist Party… Mr Crawford.'

'I was, but I had to leave,' said Crawford, after accepting some water, spooned into his mouth by his other captor.

'Don't lie to us Mr Crawford. We are quite capable of checking the veracity of your statements.'

'I had to leave. I didn't have a choice – really…'

'Why?'

'I shagged the party secretary and the treasurer,' he said, insouciantly, with a markedly downbeat tone of voice.

Crawford just caught the tiniest trace of a titter from the

figure behind him but the man managed to cover it up by clearing his throat.

'Your personal problems are not relevant to this discussion. What is the name of your handler, Mr Crawford?'

'They're certainly relevant to me. The bitch only reported me, because I fuc…'

'We believe you are a Russian agent, Mr Crawford. If you co-operate with us, we will be able to help you. We can protect you and offer you a new identity and a new life. If you choose to mislead us, or frustrate our investigation, the consequences would be very serious. We will return in thirty minutes.' His interviewer was not in fact leaving Crawford alone to increase his anxiety in order to exploit it, but because he couldn't keep a straight face anymore and was afraid he might begin to laugh.

'But…'

'If you try to leave the room, you will be shot. If you attack the men guarding you, you will be shot.' Crawford could not quite believe the stupidity of the anonymous speaker's last warning, as he was clearly unable to move in any direction at all in his shackles. But he avoided pointing out the fact he was obviously helpless, in the vain hope it might shorten his incarceration. The agent continued…

'If you mislead us, or give us false information, you will be shot. If you survive the interview process you will be detained at Her Majesty's pleasure– indefinitely. If you are lucky, you may be invited to take part in a prisoner exchange and spend the rest of your days experiencing all the advantages that a revolutionary socialist society can provide – a tiny apartment block in the Moscow suburbs, with a faltering electricity supply, no hot water and a broken lift, queues for non-existent food, public transport that stinks of…'

'Please – can I have some more water, I really need to take a piss too…?'

Mary and Ian were very tense and irritable by the time they had steered their animals through the green, tree-lined gardens and ornamental parkland between Oliver's Mount and the lower slopes of the headland, where Mary had decided to part company with her reluctant charges. Pepper and Sweetie had become Grouch and Groan, though it was their human kidnappers who were entirely to blame. The donkeys marched on snacks, pats and daylight and they hadn't had either since leaving their cosy stable. It didn't help that Sweetie had kicked Ian in the shins for mishandling her bridle. Now even Mary had to admit defeat.

'No more Mary. No more,' said Ian, at the end of his tether. 'I've had enough walking and so has this bloody thing, sorry Pepp, but you're an ass – a donkey I mean.'

'All right, we'll release them here, said Mary. We've made our point.'

'Made our point!' You're mad.'

'I am not *mad*. I'm *not* mad. We've liberated them.'

'No. We've stolen them, put 'em at risk – and us I might add, and abandoned 'em at night in a friggin' park so you can boast that you're an animal rights activist. You're sick – and I'm sick of your bullshit. Here – take the bloody donkey and leave me alone!' barked Ian, storming off into the darkness.

'Ian! Come back… pleeease!' cried Mary. But Ian had already disappeared into the black depths of the night. Mary sagged and started to weep, then Pepper brought her back down to earth by shoving her off the back rest of the park bench she was resting on. Sweetie took flight while Pepper stood over Mary and stuck his nose in her lap.

'I hope you're proud of that'… snapped Mary.

Then Pepper started to relieve himself on Mary's baseball boots.

Sweetie, who had stopped further down the path, was observing a queue of other humans down below on Rope Walk, filing out of Mystery City with their tools and equipment trolleys to a line of vans on the pavements. The donkey, who was now hungry and tired, knew humans meant food, so she set off down the winding footpath towards the club, buoyed up by the smell of chips and seared onions drifting up from Ned's takeaway food caravan on the empty pay and display car park nearby.

Chapter Fifteen

This Ol' House

Seaforth House stood alone on the barren peak of Weare Topping, overlooking the northern tip of Kettleness. For eighty years it had weathered storms, sleet, snow and the occasional bleaching heats of summer, though during the last three decades it had barely been touched. Despite its neglected facade, it was endowed with all the characteristic emblems and motifs of the archetypal redbrick arts and crafts era mansion, with decorative stucco inset panels, framed in limed oak along the breadth of its upper floors, hand-carved wooden brackets, leadwork mirroring natural forms and stained glass inset panels in its windows. Seaforth also featured the largest stained glass window outside of a church in North Yorkshire which overlooked the main staircase. It was a house like no other in the region; and somewhat at odds with the huge rocks and boulder stones crowding the ground around its skirts, a testament to a forgotten era, marooned on the highest point of the North Sea coast.

The main body of the house supported two pairs of bay windows that jutted out on its longest sides, like the inboard superstructure of a battleship. The rear pair overlooked the sea and were crowned with turrets set into roofline. The front bays, by contrast, looked back over the landscape, from the rocky stones and bluffs of its near aspect to the steep green hills beyond. In its bloom, Seaforth had been among the most admired new houses in England. But in the space of sixty years, its owners, the Benedict family, had frittered away their fortune and slipped into comparative poverty and ordinariness.

To compound their misfortunes, a landslip had taken away the only access road to the old house, leaving them with no other way of reaching their family home, save a narrow gravel footpath which ran perilously close to the edge of the cliffs. Their last great asset was effectively cut off from the world. In the years since, the house had succumbed to the aggregations of time and climate, settling into a condition of romantic decay. It was now little more than a semi-derelict folly; a crumbling monument to the thwarted ambitions of a once-respected family.

Meredith Benedict would be the last permanent living occupant of the once-great house. The youngest child of Anthony and Helen Benedict, she had always loved Seaforth, the remoteness of its location, the ever-changing canvas of sea and sky and the dramatic sunsets. Although she had little in the way of human contact, she felt grateful to be living in such a wild and beautiful place, despite the many deprivations – and had decided she would stay, eking out an existence on the monthly markets, selling her embroidery, knitwear and herbal remedies, with no one for company but her three feral cats. Occasionally pawning what remained of the family's rare china, precious silverware and jewellery to pay for her coal and groceries meant she was comfortable. But there was little left to pay for anything other than essential repairs and so she restricted herself to one wing of the house, knitting during the evenings or reading books from the great library, in the fading grandeur of the dining room with only oil lamps and candles for light.

As Meredith grew old in solitude, contemplating the seasons and the passage of time, she became a recluse, taking in the gifts of food and clothing donated by her close friends and neighbours. Her garden grew tangled and wild behind the boundary walls, until the front door and the path leading to it was entirely covered by brambles and ivy.

The only way in or out that was left to her was a side door into the coal house, on the southern wing of the property. Eventually she stopped answering to callers, though her neighbours would sometimes see lights burning behind the shabby curtains, until the autumn of 1982 when the house remained cloaked in darkness for the whole winter.

Now in the spring, the locals had begun to see lights inside again, though it was never usually more than the glow of a single bulb, which burned unblinkingly throughout the night. But unknown to them, Meredith had perished the previous year, trapped in a cave by the tide at dusk; succumbing to the numbing cold of the North Sea's bitter winds. Who or what now occupied the empty rooms of the decaying old house was not yet a puzzle that required investigation. Her neighbours at High Topping Farm and Alcoves Dairy had more pressing matters to occupy their minds –the strange disappearance of several lambs and ewes, a ram, five cats, two pigs and a cockerel. High Topping Farm's Collie, Ben, had found a blood trail leading to the sea, though the scent was lost after another storm and a heavy fall of rain. But the mystery took a more sinister turn after the disappearance of two day-trippers.

On the second day of the Easter holiday, a married couple had vanished from their tent at the mouth of Ash Gill ravine during the night, leaving most of their possessions in front of the beach. It was assumed they had left on an impulse after an argument and returned home in the early hours. But against the background of the missing farm animals, their sudden absence only increased the sense of unease amongst the local population. There were tales of sink holes in the area, which were reputedly linked to caves inside the cliffs and used by smugglers hundreds of years before, though none had ever been found. If such places still existed, then no one had ever returned from them alive, and so Kettleness continued to keep its oldest secrets. After all the rumours and speculation, it took another missing cat to stir the police into action.

Councillors Jim and Eileen Halshaw had reached a point in their relationship where any thoughts of passion or physical affection had long since evaporated. Theirs was a marriage of shared chores, books, comfortable domesticity and committees, punctuated by conversations which revolved around the common topics of family, friends and the toileting habits of their pets Bell, Gemma and Bonnie – their pedigree Boxers. They were, in their own words, experienced shitologists. Firm and odourless evacuations were related throughout the Halshaw house with great glee, but runny poos were pored over – in a manner of speaking – with great seriousness and interest. Mustard-coloured smoothies or 'Mr Whippy's' were almost enough to ruin their day.

Marmalade, their ginger Tom, was large and spoiled and very rarely left the comfort of his armchair. He could no longer force his girth past the frame of the cat flap with ease after growing heavy and voluptuous on a diet of Whitby smokies, creamed rice and Harpers cat biscuits poured from the constantly replenished cardboard boxes of treats which arrived almost daily from Woolworths. In between sleeps, he lolled or spread himself unselfishly over the expensive furniture of his human carers; or in between the dogs.

It was the smell of a half-eaten portion of battered haddock that drew him outside one night, to meet his nemesis, past the open door to their back yard, where his father was emptying the dust from their coal bucket. The portly cat tracked the scent of the abandoned fish supper along their garden path to the boundary hedge, ducking down and squeezing himself through a gap in the knotted web of its lowest branches and roots. It was on the other side that he met Mr Boldwood, lurking downwind in a rusting, perforated bathtub, which had once served as the drinking trough for the milking herd but now lay abandoned on a cracked, compacted ribbon of mud, fifty yards from their boundary fence.

Marmalade's last breaths were painful and short, swung violently from side to side, until he was decapitated, between the upper and lower jaws of a beast that had no business wandering the lanes and fields of rural North Yorkshire, or any other earthly place. Like Marmalade, Mr Boldwood's first live prey – as a werewolf, had been his own pet cat Bagshott. Since when he had polished off a whole street's worth of feline victims, before moving onto rams, ewes, saddleback pigs and the occasional human as a main, if the opportunity presented itself. But cats remained his favourite starter, though the human side of him had not yet come to terms with the giant hairballs in the toilet bowl the following afternoon.

The same evening, Boldwood had slaughtered the three

Turkish kitchen staff at Crescent Moon on Pilger Street in his native Cloughton. But he had not been able to repeat the carnage in the front of the takeaway, thanks to the quick thinking of the owner; who had thrown a catering size HP Sauce bottle into his jaws in panic. Once his fangs had torn open the plastic squeezy bottle and the contents had filled his mouth, Boldwood couldn't get back to the river fast enough. Something furry and light, with small crunchy bones was just the tonic he needed to dislodge the dreadful memory of the hot brown sauce. Although Marmalade was a little bigger than his usual entrées, he was at least very furry.

Chapter Sixteen

Police and Thieves

Superintendent d'Ascoyne wasted no time hunting down Inspector Marshall before he had a chance to escape the station, once their Monday morning briefing had finished, pulling him into his office to pass on the Chief Constable's instructions, and reinforce his orders as to how he was to proceed with his investigation. The new protocols did not go down well with his best maverick detective.

'We can't do this properly, sealed up and stuck in the station, sir; these people need to see the locations where these attacks occurred. Then we can have some kind of meaningful discussion. How long will they stay?' he asked, referring to the Home Office representatives and the MI5 officers they had been ordered to accommodate.

'I've no idea, but we can't dictate to them what happens and where. They're…'

'In charge?'

'I didn't say that.'

'You said as much this morning, sir…'

'I did not.'

'Sir, with respect.., we've never had any proper criminal investigation start without the investigating team visiting the scene of the crime. It's a fundamental part of good casework!

They've got to see the locations of these shootings– and the context.'

'I can't overrule the Home Secretary. It'll be the end of my career. And yours.'

'He's a cabinet minister, sir. They're certainly no friends of people like us. I don't much like being patted on the head and told how to do my job by a lot of politicians and trigger-happy goons in suits who think they're on a higher plane of intelligence. If I'm still in charge, then we do it my way. We go to the crime scenes, whether the press are there or not, then we have a meeting. We'll find nowt sat on our lazy arses in the bloody station.'

D'Ascoyne bridled at the remark but decided to say nothing. He was hoping to shorten their encounter by allowing his inspector to blow hot and cold. But Inspector Marshall wasn't going to be cowed.

'We do things the way we always do them. Or you can take me off the case. I can't see how they can reasonably object to being shown the scene of the crime; they must have some flexibility of approach.'

'You're not going to stir things up, Ray?'

'I'm not sitting on my bloody hands, smiling sweetly with my trap shut, like a nun at a strip club, sir. If it's my investigation, we do it the right way. Our investigation – our rules. Just remember sir, if this goes tits up, you can bet your arse we'll get put in the frame. The Home Office and MI5 aren't going to carry the can if they can fit us up. We do it the right way then there's no comeback.'

'Don't do anything. Until I speak to the Chief Constable.'

'What's wrong with talking to these people when they arrive?'

'They're already here – so I'm told. I don't want you to…'

'What?'

'Make a scene? Oh come on Super…'

'Will you just *try* for once Ray…?'

'How did your meeting with the Chief go on Saturday?'

'It was… *cordial*…'

'We could always send our visitors for a Mexican, sir.'

'That's not funny. They were all back on duty yesterday – after the food poisoning episode I trust?'

'Everyone on the roster, sir. Just a bit pink about the cheeks. Both sets…'

'Didn't we apprehend a reporter interfering with the crime scene?'

'Yes sir. Wolfie Crawford. All in my report.'

'Where is he, did we caution him?'

'We took him to A&E with our walking wounded sir, as he was unconscious when he was found. Apparently he was *discharged* by our lot into the custody of four men from the Home Office who just appeared by magic after he was checked by the doctors. They wheeled him out handcuffed to a patient transport trolley into a white Transit – Moyne said he was more or less forced to sign the custody transfer document by two Security Service goons packing holsters. The van had a sandwich escort, high performance BMW saloons front an' back. They set off like Niki Lauda with James Hunt on his arse. We haven't heard a thing from them since they bloody kidnapped him.'

'Where are you going now Marshall?'

'George and I are following up a lead, sir. I'm not sure it's going to amount to anything, but there's nothing else in my in tray so we'll take a sniff.'

'Just make sure you're back for two o'clock, for the next meeting at 2.30. I want us to look as though we know what we're doing.'

Chapter Seventeen

At the Kenwith Valley Gorge Museum

Derek decided to called Alan Chipping, his contact at the museum.

'Alan, it's me... I thought I'd try and catch you early.'

'Derek! Hello... I was wondering when you'd be in touch.'

'I've been keeping my head down over the past few days, for obvious reasons. Are you alone there?'

Alan leant back in his swivel chair, as much as he dared without toppling over, to check the next two aisles in the archive room.

'I think so, yes. Fairly certain, it's just me and the cleaners at the moment – do you have news?'

'This isn't the time to be flippant.'

'I wasn't being flippant, I can hardly justify being jocular can I? Working on the fringes of a war zone, if you're on edge it's hardly fair to take it out on me, so – can we start again..? Do you have news?'

'I'm sorry Alan, I'm a little tense.'

'Apology accepted... may I repeat my question again?'

'Yes of course. I do have some news of sorts, depending on whether you believe in curses,' he muttered.

'Curses? Are you sure? Is this about your *find*?'

'Yes, it is about *the find*. According to your very generously-proportioned friend Lawrence, there are *two* curses attached to it. Most historical objects that are considered unlucky usually make do with one, so that was a pleasant surprise. He didn't want to touch it with anything greasier than his napkin. It's cost me half a day and a restaurant bill that I'm still in awe of, to find out I've made a discovery that no one wants to touch.'

'Well, thank you for letting me know. One of those coins is at my house. What did he tell you about this curse?'

'Only that anyone who comes into possession of it dies within the year,' said Derek, uneasily, 'according to those historians who've studied its origins. I for one would be very pleased to hear an alternative viewpoint, though at the moment that doesn't seem very likely to be forthcoming.'

'Can I call you back later?' asked the historian, beginning to fret.

'It won't make any difference if you disposed of it, sold it or lost it Alan,' said Derek brutally. 'If you've handled it, the end result is the same. I don't know where we go from here. I just thought I'd do you the courtesy of letting you know. If only your colleague had been as candid with me, before he ate a hundred and eighty pounds worth of game and vegetables at my expense.'

'I wish I'd never touched that coin.'

'Did you hear what I said Alan?'

'Yes, yes... I'm sorry, I just drifted away there for a second,' he explained, still stunned. 'What on earth did you order for goodness' sake?'

'Soup, stew and apple tart, though I can't repeat the names of the dishes your friend stuffed himself with. I couldn't even read most of the language on the damn menu – it was all in French.'

'I feel a little guilty now Derek. I'd forgotten he had such an appetite.'

'It's not your fault he eats for three. With a little adjustment I should be able to put it on the partner's expense account, but that's the least of my problems at the moment. I don't expect you come across much in the way of cursed relics – do you Alan?'

'Not usually, no.'

'I can offer you an amulet,' added Derek, abruptly.

'An amulet? *You*– give *me,* an *amulet?*'

'Yes… an amu…'

'I know what an amulet is. We've got five or six trays full of the damn things in the archive. I had no idea you were interested in things like that.'

'I'm not, well I don't… sorry…' said Derek, stumbling over his words. 'Strictly speaking, it's just not something I'm comfortable divulging. My mother used to make charms and my father swore by them,' he said, lying with a fluency that only a man of the law could fake. 'My aunt made – pardon me –*makes* them too. I've always worn one,' he said, imagining his hands around the neck of Violet Penrose.

'Derek, you really are an enigma.'

'Mine gives me peace of mind.'

'Yes, you do lead rather a charmed life, don't you? If you're offering to give me one, I certainly won't refuse it. Where does she live, your aunt?'

'If you'd like me to get you one, then I'll bring it to you. She doesn't like people visiting. It sets her off.'

'Sets her off… Sets off her what?'

'She has to spend hours cleaning other people's energies out of her house, she says. Muttering things with hazel twigs and a candle.'

'Can amulets protect against curses? Aren't curses more powerful?'

'Look, I'll drop it off as soon as I can. I don't think you need to worry too much at the moment.'

'That's all right for you to say. I'm not going to sleep tonight.'

Shaking The Tree

Marshall and Broadhead visit Derek Beautimann

'Right George. Let's go and visit your favourite law firm and speak to Mr Beautimann.'

'Are they open today? It's Bank Holiday Monday,' added Broadhead, tutting.

'His firm offer people legal advice to the under 25s for a set fee today. Their way of "giving something back" to the community. Quite nice of them actually, though they do get a lot of publicity for it. It's the only day of the year you'll get a cheap tip at BB&T.'

'They won't like us turning up on the off-chance.'

'Don't you think so George? Do you know – that never crossed my mind,' grinned Marshall,' but as we need to speak to him in working hours, we'll not be able to wait until he's gone home, will we? It'll be a nice excuse to see Shirley anyway,' said Marshall, referring to the receptionist at Beautimann, Buerk and Trippe. 'She's a very nice lady, unlike the er, partners – and very nicely turned out,' he beamed, roguishly.

'Are we walking?'

'We certainly are, waste of a good pair of shoes taking the car.'

Beautimann Buerk and Trippe kept offices in a large

mansion block on Plantagenet Place, overlooking a small park enclosed by railings where office workers took their lunch breaks and the residents of the other buildings nearby went to read or exercise. The law firm occupied three floors above ground level, though the basement held a small cafe called Six Steps, which was popular with students and artists and was named after the number of steps it took to enter from the pavement above.

Inspector Marshall took off his old hat as he walked in through the open front door of BB&T, turned left and strode bumptiously into reception, hanging back momentarily to hold open the half-glazed door for his sergeant. Marshall winked at the duty receptionist, resting his forearms on the top of the tall counter. 'Hello love,' he said cheerfully, leaning cheekily over the divide. 'I've come to see Mr Beautimann. Could you tell him Inspector Marshall and Detective Sergeant Broadhead would like to ask him a few questions. Shirley not in today?' he asked, looking carefully for any sort of adverse reaction from the woman behind the typewriter. Broadhead stood slightly behind and to the side of his superior, wearing his best withering gaze as they tried to unsettle their prey.

'Do you have an appointment, Inspector?' asked Maureen, smiling back, though her smile was more of a grimace. The muscles in her face were twitching and her eyes appeared to be flitting from one point in the room to another, in a poor attempt to avoid being locked into the laser beam-like gaze of the two policemen.

'We're on official business love. So the answer's no.'

A young man who was seated by the coffee table raised his newspaper to cover his eyes.

'OH, HELLO TOM!' said Marshall loudly. Hope you're keeping yourself out of trouble lad?'

'Yes sir, Mr Marshall,' replied the thing behind the *Whitborough Evening News*.

'I'll see if he's still with his client,' said Maureen, reaching for the phone. 'Actually, I'll go upstairs and check with him in person, Inspector,' she continued, thinking fast, 'there's been a fault on his extension today, interference or something… Could you wait here please?'

'A fault on the line! Better get that sorted out then, eh?' said Broadhead with a hint of sarcasm.

'I'll just be a minute…' said Maureen, hobbling around the edge of the counter to the door in her three-inch heels.

'How women manage to walk in shoes like that I'll never know,' said Marshall drily. 'What does your missus put on her feet George?'

'I don't take much notice in all honesty guv.'

'She doesn't totter from one room to another like that one though does she?'

'No. Except on Friday nights. She wears these strappy heel things to Mecca. I said to her she was gonna break her bloody ankle on their steps one night, but I don't think she appreciated the advice.'

'No, they never take it in the way it's meant, do they? Wives… they always think you're picking on them. Vera just wears her slippers all the time now anyway. Except when she goes to the doc's in her pumps… George?'

'What?'

'Have a peek about…do you see any CCTV in here? Go over to the door and stick your foot against it – keep an eye

131

out for anyone coming down,' hissed Marshall. 'I'm going to have a peek at the register.'

'Nothing for you to see lad,' growled Broadhead, as the *Whitborough Evening News* was lowered to reveal the top half of Tom Hutchinson's face before it was swiftly raised to conceal it once again.

'Marshall reached over the counter and picked up the appointments diary and Maureen's crib sheet-cum-jotter pad.'

'Guv – there's two pairs of legs at the top of the stairs. It's her and a male. Could be Beautimann.'

'Are they moving?'

'No. I think they're arguing…'

'Arguing? How d'you know that,' said Marshall, running his eyes over Maureen's notes.

'They're waving their hands about.'

'Can you see their faces?'

'Nothing from the neck up, the ceiling void from the next staircase is in the way.'

'And where d'you think you're going?' asked Marshall, glaring accusingly at the young man on the benches who had just stood up and grabbed his bag.'

'I just remembered I have to meet somebody Mr Marshall,' he said sheepishly. 'I forgot.'

'Sit back down and cover your face up, you little shit,' snapped the policeman, 'or you'll soon find out what an angry copper can do with a document stapler.'

'Sorry,' mumbled Tom, sitting back resentfully on the red leather bench cushion.

'Hurry up guv, the bloke is trying to pull away, you'll have about four or five seconds once he starts moving.'

'I wonder what his legal sec's doing on reception..?' asked Marshall, tapping the countertop gently with his fingertips as he ran his eyes over Maureen's scribblings. Then a folded sheet of plain paper fell out between the pages. It was covered in calculations and small sums made up of multiple figures, which Marshall guessed were connected to a list of high value item purchases, as might be imagined by someone who is expecting to come into a large sum of money. The items were written randomly in several places, each word was appended with a question mark and comprised the following: New car? House? Cruise ship holiday? Splurge in London? Nose job? New tits?

'Ah-ha!'

On the reverse side was a sketch of a very ostentatious antique ring – and a gold coin.

'They're moving guv!'

Inspector Marshall span the open diary around and placed it back down on the other side of the divide in one smooth movement, then he put the jotter pad back in its place just as Derek and Maureen reached the bottom of the stairs. Marshall stepped back from the counter and picked up a folding calendar from the leather table mat further down, so he had something else in his hand as the solicitor and his junior colleague entered the waiting room.

'When's the Super's birthday?' asked Marshall, replacing the calendar again as nonchalantly as he could to disguise his intentions. 'Hello Mr Beautimann – we'd like to talk to you if we may – about a matter of mutual interest.'

'Is this an official visit, Inspector? This is our annual charity day.'

'Unofficially official sir.'

'Oh. Well we can do this in here in that case,' said Derek, indicating the door to a small side office, playing for a few seconds grace. My legal secretary will join us.'

'As you wish sir, unless you'd prefer me to speak to you privately.'

'Oh? To what end?'

'I'd like the benefit of your advice sir, as one professional to another. Regarding a matter of mutual interest.'

'Those words again…' said Derek slowly, 'but I'm quite sure I've no idea what you mean, Inspector.'

'Man to man…' replied Marshall, grinning infectiously and ignoring his host's request for clarity.

'This is very er – irregular. Am I to understand you wish me to give of myself for free?'

'Call it what you like Mr Beautimann,' replied Marshall cockily, smiling broadly again, as he pushed himself up onto his toes. I'm not going to cross your palm with silver, *or gold…* if you get my drift,' said Marshall, dropping a very large metaphorical pebble into Derek's metaphorical glassy pond. There was a very distinct glug from the throat of the solicitor, as his Adam's apple reset itself.

'Would you like to come through?' asked Derek, opening the door of the tiny office for the inspector and his colleague with a nervous air. 'Maureen – would you give us ten minutes?'

'Well gentlemen, what can I do for you? It's always a pleasure to see our friends in the police,' he said without irony. Detective Sergeant Broadhead had never felt more tempted to comment but restrained himself in deference to his inspector who was about to spike the solicitor's guns.

'Do you get out much in the evenings sir..?'

134

'What do you mean exactly, Inspector?'

'Any outdoor hobbies… pastimes… Would you say you were the outdoor type?'

'Why do you ask?'

'Are you familiar with the plateau above Cayton Bay, Mr Beautimann?'

'Only as much as anyone else is in Whitborough, Inspector.'

'Have you been there recently, Mr Beautimann?'

'During the evening sir,' added DS Broadhead, 'after dark…?'

'Can I ask what your interest is exactly?'

'Well sir, two of our officers were witnesses to a very unusual get-together a few nights ago at that very location. They both identified you as the conductor of some kind of er… *ceremony*– not that there's anything illegal in practising… whatever it was you were practising. But I'd like to know if you saw anybody else in the general area acting suspiciously…'

The two policemen were trying so hard not to smirk and erupt into shrieks of laughter that it must have looked as though they were suffering some kind of nervous facial cramp.

'Is something the matter, Inspector?' asked Derek, feeling very uncomfortable.

'Sorry sir… itchy nose. George and I…*that is*…Detective Sergeant Broadhead and myself, are very sensitive to pollen. We get terrible hay fever. I think it's come early this year.'

'The two policemen to whom you were referring are fully recovered then are they, Inspector?' asked Derek, trying to buy himself some time to think.'I read that they were suffering from hallucinations and delusions after being bitten by adders and a swarm of wasps. If that had happened to any of us we'd probably be seeing pink elephants, so their recollections of the night in question are open to all kinds of interpretations, wouldn't you say?'

'A very sensible summary sir and a very plausible viewpoint. Very reasonable. Fluent even, wouldn't you say George?'

'Very fluent,' added Detective Sergeant Broadhead, deadpan, looking at a smudge on his finger with disgust after rubbing his teeth.

'Is something the matter?'asked Beautimann, fascinated by the detective sergeant's demeanour.

'Greenfly…' replied Broadhead, wiping his finger very slowly on the solicitor's blotter.

'So– you weren't actually present at this gathering sir?' asked Marshall. 'Is that what you're saying?'

'I don't wish to comment, Inspector, because I'm not particularly interested and I happen to be quite busy,' though he was trying hard to ignore the sight of the horrible greenish yellow smudge on his blotter which seemed to be mixed with tiny seed husks. Broadhead gave him an unfriendly fixed grin.

Satisfied he now had his man exactly where he wanted him, Marshall went for the kill. 'It's just we've got two other witnesses who are willing to swear you were in Cayton Bay last Monday night in your dressing gown with your prayer cap on, brawling with someone who was a dead ringer for the Milk Tray man would you like to comment on that?'

Chapter Eighteen

Police on My Back

The George Cayley conference room at Whitborough Police Station, where the first meeting between the police, the Home Office, MI5 and the Navy was just getting under way, was named after the Yorkshire-born pioneer of flight,though no title, or scheme of works, could ever hope to redeem its horrible interior. It had no natural light, character, or ambience and always produced a profoundly negative effect on the dispositions of anyone forced to endure its claustrophobic atmosphere for more than an hour.

A square, inward-facing, fixed seating arrangement compounded the dreadful laboratory-like atmosphere and forced its guests into rigid adversarial positions. Even the lecterns were bolted to the floor, like the rows of benches beneath the departure boards at major railway stations. The Cayley Room was the antithesis of every principle of Feng Shui and was universally disliked by everyone who was forced to use it.

Two feeble extractor fans could barely cope with the smog of half a packet of Benson and Hedges, six of which had already been shared by Marshall and Broadhead, who were contemplating their recent visit to the offices of Beautimann, Buerk and Trippe, before Superintendent d'Ascoyne rose to introduce himself and his inspector at the lectern.Half an hour and another six Benson and Hedges later, Marshall closed the incident file and his talk on the week's events and returned to his reserved place on the benches. A handful of spare chairs had been brought in, in an attempt to make the room layout less rigid, but it only added to the general discomfort by forcing people to twist around on their seats. The room remained quiet for a few seconds and then James Stocke, the senior man from the MI5 delegation, rose and walked over to the projector screen wall.

'Thank you for your excellent briefing, Inspector. It's always refreshing for us in the Security Service to be able to work alongside the Police Service, the armed forces and the other departments of state,' he said, nodding towards the Home Office team and the two senior Royal Navy officers.

'We shall now reveal what *we* know, in order to ensure you all have a full picture of the situation here. This information is highly classified and will remain so for many more years after this meeting and of course you've all signed the Official Secrets Act,' he continued, before taking a deep breath. His opening statement was quite a surprise…

'There are ten KGB sleeper agents in Whitborough-on-Sea, gentlemen. Six of them, we suspect, have had special training with their Spetsnaz special forces. These people are here to disable our facility at Staxton Wold, in the event of a war.

Seven have regular jobs, in the public sector, in transport and utilities. The command pair work in agriculture, because farms are much more difficult to monitor, as we all know from the experiences of our people on the Irish border. I'll come to the big fish last,' he said, pausing a moment to look into the eyes of the Home Office delegation once more.

'Our homegrown Ivans have been a peaceful lot until recently, but since the first Monday of the month there has been a marked increase in the volume and frequency of their communications, correlating directly with the deterioration in East-West relations. Our analysis of the attack on HMS *Brazen* has concluded that this is a clear signal the USSR is preparing for war with NATO and has activated its agents in the west. We can expect many more of these incidents in the weeks ahead.'

'This year, other allies of the USSR have been assisting the arming of the IRA, the INLA and WRA to put an extra strain on our resources at home and to take our attention and dissipate our forces in this time of increasing tension.'

'The WRA?' said Marshall. *'Who the bloody hell are they?'*

'The Welsh Republican Army, Inspector. A small but significantly militant minority.'

'Hol-idday cott-edge arrrson-ests witha grudge, d'yew mean d'yew?' added the second Home Office liaison Huw Griffiths, sardonically.

'We also know they're establishing a racketeering operation in the borough, using minor players from the Republican movement and a pool of doormen from Belfast and Glasgow,' continued Stocke, ignoring the jibe from the Welsh civil servant.

Marshall decided the time had come to offer his own opinion on MI5's revelation, before the moment had passed.

'I'm not sure whether we should now feel privileged or flattered, that you've shared this intel with us at last, because up until today we've been kept in ignorance of information which would certainly have been essential to the wellbeing of our people,' bemoaned Marshall sarcastically. Superintendent d'Ascoyne crossed his legs and looked despairingly into the black mirrors of his shoes, from his detached chair.

'This type of information is shared only by the Security Service, Inspector; under normal circumstances, on a need-to-know basis. The classification rating would normally restrict its disclosure to anyone outside the Intelligence Services, to prevent it escaping into the public domain.'

'I should point out that we have all taken a similar oath to the Security Service in the police. And we take the same risks… racketeering certainly comes under our responsibility.'

'We appreciate your efforts to protect the public, Inspector, but this is the way the game is played.'

'It may be *a game* to *you and your colleagues*– but it's been life or death for us this last week. Which farm?' asked Marshall, with deadly seriousness, demanding a response.

'I beg your pardon, Inspector?'

D'Ascoyne put his hand over his eyes and the bridge of his nose.

'Which farm is it that's kept by these bloody KGB goons?'

'As the inspector has so recently signed the Official Secrets Act, and is "on side" I think we can justify disclosure,' said one of the men from the Home Office. 'Let the inspector see the first page summary. We can't let you have a copy, Inspector, but you're welcome to read the particular page we've highlighted in orange.'

A shallow black box file made its way down the line from the Home Office team to Inspector Marshall via their civil servants and the Royal Navy. Marshall opened the lid and studied the contents.

'Only the top leaf, Inspector – thank you. We'll take it back as soon as you've read it please.'

'Manor Farm, well that's a surprise…' said Marshall with angry exasperation and a large dollop of sarcasm.

'Inspector?'

'Manor Farm,' he repeated, locking eyes with Superintendent d'Ascoyne, who puckered his mouth as if to speak, but clammed up in the interests of self-preservation.

'That's correct,' added the older agent, trying to read the invisible communication between Inspector Marshall and his superior.

'How long have you been watching the place?' Marshall asked, still staring at his chief.

'On a daily basis, nearly a year. Since the last Warsaw Pact manoeuvres.'

'Not since the last bloody war started though have you?' snorted Marshall disrespectfully. 'So you won't know about the Hoopers then and their secret arms dump!' he snapped, breaking off his accusing glare to stare at the smoke-stained tiles on the suspended ceiling.

'Arms dump?'

'The munitions they stole, during the war.'

'Munitions?'

'Munitions! Guns!' shouted Marshall. 'Things that go *BANG!* A bloody Heinkel bomber crash-landed on their land in the war. When my predecessors got to it, the guns had been stripped out and two of the bombs were gone. They've never been recovered. The Hooper brothers were in the frame for it but the authorities couldn't find the weapons. They never found the bloody grenades, or the rifles, or the Bren guns they nicked from the Home Guard either. It was all forgotten after the war. But some of our other crims who dared to cross swords with the Hoopers certainly saw them. Somebody who didn't want to go on the record said Vernon Hooper had gone to the Mill Inn one night and fired a burst at the racks and optics behind the bar with one of those German MG's. Then turned a one-armed bandit to scrap with another.'

'Why is this not in the file?' asked the head of the Home Office delegation, looking to his junior colleagues.

'The terms of reference that dictated the scope of the report only bracketed the post-war period sir. We…'

'Then *we* haven't got the complete picture have *we*?' snapped their boss.

'It is very thorough, within the terms of refer…'

'You didn't think to look *outside* these terms of reference to include any pertinent facts that might put a completely different perspective on the rest of the evidence gathered?'

'We were told to concentrate only on intelligence and evidence after 1950, sir. *The instruction from your office.*'

'And you call yourself Intelligence officers,' said Marshall, flinging his chewing gum in the basket. 'I hope to God the rest of you are up to scratch, or we'll all be working for bloody Brezhnev by 1984.'

'You're suspended Marshall.'

'I'm WHAT!'

'Would you like some time alone, gentlemen?' asked Superintendent d'Ascoyne, enjoying the discord in the room. 'The Inspector and I are just leaving for a moment. I will be back shortly.'

Chapter Nineteen

It's a Long Way to the Top

The pubs of Sandside and Bleake Passage, around the vicinity of Mystery City, began to fill rapidly after opening time on Easter Monday, drawing in the students and live music fans who usually filled the bars and pubs in and around the town centre. They were joined by a large number of weekenders and visitors from York, Leeds and West Yorkshire, who added at least another fifty people to the local audience.

'Make shure Jamesy's off the sauce agayne the neet. The darft sod pessed hez brichts orn Sat urr day… Where's that c**t Marek?' grumbled Barnett, looking at the empty DJ's island for his dashing eastern European disc jockey, Marek Musolov.

'There's plenty of time, Barnett. This thing doesn't start till seven,' said Paula, his bar manager.

'Quarter tae five? Aye, right enuff… Another hour afore the wee c***s start cummen enn,' moaned her boss, by way of an apology. 'Bastard cudd come early one o' thees nights. These decks daynt look after thurr selves.'

'He cleans them when he turns the lights on. When the lights are on full beam. While you're getting pissed at the bar.'

'S'whart ah like aboot hew Paula, yull nay take nonn o' marr shite.'

'*Piss off* Crosbie.'

'Gee ush a kess…'

At seven o'clock the doors opened on the unloved warm-up band, Apache Dreamland, who plugged in and started a first and final soundcheck, as best they could, with the help of some of the more experienced members of the sound crew. After a nervous ten minutes they crashed through their first song, a cover of the Ramones' 'Indian Giver' and then stopped briefly, relieved to have got through their first number without tripping over, then they tore into two of their own tunes, 'Life's Shit' and 'Girls on Buses'.

'What kind o' focken shite es thess?' drawled Barnett, firing an ash-laden tab end into the bottle bin with a practised flick.'

'They're the anarchy band Barn,' groaned Paula.'They've come from Burniston. It's their first gig, so don't be mean.'

'Make shure th'dumb barstards pay thurr drenks tab. Dedd they stump up tae play yet, by the way?'

'Are you charging them to play here?' You tightwad!'

'*Too focken right!* Thirtay bloody quedd's nort nearlay enuff fo' thess focken torture. Next time it'll be twice as focken much. Scruffy c***s sound like Tommy Cooper fallen' o'er a row o' focken dustbenns!'

After their sixth song, their singer Big Mark decided to tell a joke about the Easter Passover but lost his place in the narrative when a Pils bottle flew past his ear, narrowly missing the drummer's head.

'*No focken jokes aboot the focken Chuch!*' yelled Barnett. 'Yurve gort five focken mennetts preck…'

The compere for the Battle of the Bands contest, was well-known local funny man Ted Knight, the nearly man of North Yorkshire's club scene, whose CV flirted with the great and good of the 1950s, 60s and 70s cabaret. Ted could supply anecdotes and stories for any occasion, from the reign of Alma Cogan to the Bay City Rollers and always wore the costume of a Las Vegas cabaret singer. When he heard he was going into the black pit of Mystery City, he knew there was only one outfit that was going to save his bacon. His eye-meltingly loud Royal Stewart tartan suit, red shirt, white dickie bow tie and black suede brothel creepers which drew every eye still capable of focusing to his feet, like west coast midges to a naked leg. Ted strode out into the spotlight, licked his lips and launched. They were going to be a tough crowd, so he decided to park his more polite routine and go straight for the throat.

'RIGHT..! SHUT YER GOBS.., AN' GUARD YER DRINKS! Because *right now, boys and girls*–behind the stage… in the wings…there's a clever young fella from Yorkshire Coastal FM, to introduce our first act tonight for the 1983 Whitborough Battle of the Bands. May I present, THE SULTAN OF SOUND, THE…

'VERUCA OF VINYL!' yelled a gang of spiky students.

'…TITAN OF TAPES! DARREN DUKE!'announced Ted, through a smartly-disguised grimace. He was heard to mutter the word 'tit' soon afterwards, through the side of his mouth in the style of a bad ventriloquist.

'The titan of tapes? What kind of a bloody name is that? PRINCE OF PISS!' shouted another drunk.

'GOOD EVENING WHITBOROUGH!' shouted Darren, grinning cheesily as he skipped and hopped over the boards of the stage, in a desperate attempt to win over his audience with a cheesy pirouette and a wink.

'PISS OFF BARRY!'shouted a wag in the crowd.

'My name's Darren,' protested the DJ, still grinning, though the corners of his smile had gained some tautness, and he was starting to look more and more uncomfortable in front of the less than adoring crowd.

'PISS OFF GORDON!' yelled another wit.

'GORDON IS A MORON! GORDON IS A...'

'EH NOW! A BITTA RESPECT IN THE CHEAP SEATS... WE'RE VERY LUCKY TO HAVE YORKSHIRE COASTAL FM HERE TO SUPPORT THIS EVENT. SO SHOW SOME BLOODY MANNERS...'shouted Ted, slapping down the hecklers, though it only seemed to increase their irritation and impatience.

'WAYNE!'

A large gang of sharply-dressed new wave teens began to sing, leading in the rest of the audience. 'GET YER MULLET OFF THE STAGE, GET YER MULLET OFF THE STAGE – IF YA WON'T GET YER MULLET OFF THE STAGE, WE'LL TELL THE COPS YER BIRD'S UNDER-AGE!'

'SAD BASTARD!'

'Trying his best to smile and laugh – like he was in on the teasing – Ted put his hands together and gave the audience a slow clap, returning his microphone swiftly to his chin before anyone launched another verbal barb. 'RIGHT DARREN, WHO'S THE SECOND ACT FOR THIS BUNCH OF TWATS?'

'THE SECOND ACT is... THE CARD CHEATS.'

'WELL LET'S GET 'EM UP 'ERE, THREE CHEERS EVERYBODY! FOR THE CARD CHEATS! THANK YOU DARREN! GET 'EM ON!'

The two hosts rushed off into the safety of the wings, and then turned back to watch the second band pick up their instruments.

'I thought you said you'd done this before,' said Ted sharply, looking down on his protégé while he counted out a wad of notes in a brown envelope.

'Of course I have! But they're all punks and greasers, bloody smart arse students and Goths. They're not my audience, I play the Top 40.'

'You play the same shite as Radio One you mean. What's the point of that? You could be playing The Everlys or the Beach Boys, Elvis, Hank Williams. Now that's REAL music. An' I don't care if they're not your audience. A professional copes with any crowd. You gave up after the first heckle. You do that in the clubs, and you're dead. Where's your mettle? You're as wet as a friggin' turbot, 'an about as limp. Just stay out the bloody way until you can keep it up.'

'People are generally friendlier to me on the radio. At the very least they're polite. I'm not a damn comedian. What do you mean – keep it up?'

'Too bloody right you're not… What were they shouting about your girlfriend?'

'She's seventeen – we've known each oth…'

'SEVENTEEN? You dirty bastard. You can keep it up for a bloody teenager can't ya?'

'I'm twenty-two!'

At the front of the stage, the first band on the bill, the Card Cheats, were plugged in and taking up position. Simon, the drummer, tested his cymbals; then the singer and guitarist Jesse struck the strings of his Telecaster to prime the crowd.

Cassandra, their bass player counted in the first song then kicked a plastic pint glass of stale water in the direction of two brothers who were trying to look up her tartan miniskirt.

'WE'RE THE CARD CHEATS. WE DO POP SONGS IN A PUNK STYLE. This is our first number. Rah Rah RASPUTINNN! Get the bloody beers in…'

Outside on Rope Walk, the queue was growing down the seagull-soiled pavements.

'Can't come in wi'chips…' said Ian Dowson, one of Barnett's weekend doormen, manhandling a woozy-looking youth with shaggy hair aside from the front entrance, guiding him onto the kerb to test his balance.

'YOU SELL CHIPS INSIDE!' he half-shouted, stumbling backwards off the pavement, dropping some of his food in the road.

'Dump 'em or eat 'em then piss off. *Ya barred!*' said Ian, as the young man sloped off, sulking, zigzagging unsteadily down the old flagstones that covered the narrow back road from the club.

'Can I take this in?' asked another young girl timidly, offering a half-eaten pitta bread for inspection.

'No kebabs inside luv.'

'There's no meat in it – I'm a vegetarian…'

'No kebabs. They get trod in t'carpets. Finish it off then you can come in. NEXT!' he shouted, moving the girl aside into the 'corral', a roped-off area for people wanting some fresh air and quiet or respite from the smoky, raucous crush of bodies inside.

'Move along, steady. Keep moving.'… ordered Simon Akin, Ian's partner on the door, ushering more youngsters onto the edge of the vestibule. 'Get yer money out!'

'Can we get student discount?'asked Connor Knowles, holding up his Student Union card for the withering eyes of the doormen.

'KIOSK…' groaned Ian, pointing a meaty finger at Martine in the admittance booth. 'See Martine or Paula,' he added brusquely, avoiding any further eye contact.

Outside the utility, where the door staff went to smoke and loiter, Brandon Kirk, Barnett's head doorman, took another mouthful of Clausthaler alcohol-free lager and pressed his tongue against the roof of his mouth, as he tried to form an opinion of its flavour. Sweetie, Mary Shipley's misbehaving donkey, kicked out from her hiding place, hidden in an alcove of empty beer kegs and pallets, cracking the flux seal on the gas main.

'All right then! Who's in the second-class shaggers'suite?' shouted Brandon, at the source of the noise, expecting to find a couple of sheepish teenagers with their trousers around their ankles.'

'EEEAWWWWWWW!'

'The donkey charged, just as Brandon stepped forwards, taking the doorman by surprise, knocking him off his feet as she trotted off towards the scent of the night air drifting in from Rope Walk.

Chapter Twenty

Tuesday Morning

Lindsay Boldwood had finally elected to visit his local surgery in Scalby to try and identify the cause of his lost evenings, once he had visited the Job Centre in Whitborough to leave a card for the new staff vacancies. He had no more bookings in the week after Easter, which offered him a short window of opportunity in which to interview potential replacements– in time for the summer season. His formerly loyal young helpers had suddenly resigned and fled to the comparative safety of their respective college towns, never to return. There were five GPs on duty on the day of his visit, and as he didn't have a particular favourite, being a very rare visitor to the surgery, he elected to see the first doctor available, Doctor Waller. Their conversation was brief but cordial and went exactly like this:

'I think I've had a blackout...or blackouts.'

'Oh? What makes you think that?'

'Well, I was indoors and...'

'At your hotel?'

'Yeah, at the hotel. I remember feeling really hot and itchy – this funny feeling I've been getting. It just comes on me all of a sudden; then I seem to have some kind of swoon. *The next thing I know*, I wake up with no memory of what I've done. Sometimes, I've woken up without my clothes on. I've ripped them all off,' he said, twisting the truth. 'It's hard to describe…'

'You have no memory of taking them off?'

'No I don't. It happened late afternoon, well, early evening, on two consecutive nights, at the end of the month.'

'All your clothes?'

'Aye,' said Boldwood cautiously. 'I don't particularly relish waking up in the buff in my profession – for obvious reasons. I'm not running a nudist colony.'

'Is there any history of sleepwalking in your family?'

'No.'

'Have we ever taken your blood pressure Lindsay?' asked Waller, attempting to displace his anxiety.

'No, I know it was high for a while…'

'Well we can do that today. If you've got no objections?'

'No. I've got no objections Doctor.'

'Any history of epilepsy, fits?'

'EPILEPSY! I bloody hope not!'

'Well…as your doctor, I have to consider everything. But it's far more likely – if it is your blood pressure – that it's low enough or high enough to cause you to swoon, though that still wouldn't explain the torn clothing of course. You can develop epilepsy at any time in life, but it's not the end of the world if you do. You'd just have to adjust to your new circumstances; it's just one possible explanation Lindsay.'

'Can you give me something for it… if I have it, that is?'

'Yes, we can prescribe sodium valproate. It's not a cure, but it should reduce the frequency or likelihood of any further attacks.'

'All right… I know my blood pressure is, or was, a little higher than it should be, but here's the odd thing. It's gone right down. I can't understand it.'

'So you've checked it yourself recently?'

'Yes, I have. But the funny thing is, I used to be out of breath by the time I'd got to the second floor of the pub; my ticker used to be racing by the second landing. Now, I can skip up the stairs, as nimble as a cat, and hardly break sweat. That can't be normal, can it?'

'Are you taking any kind of drug – any stimulants... amphetamines?'

'Do I look like that sort of person...?'

'I have to ask, I'm sorry.'

'No's the answer. *No I bloody DON'T.'*

'Thank you.'

'I'm sorry Doctor... I'm not normally snappy. I'm just a bit out of sorts.'

'That's all right Mr Boldwood, you're not the first person to swear in here, and you certainly won't be the last. We'll just forget that shall we? Are you taking *any* kind of medication at all? Any over the counter medicines, or natural remedies?'

'I took some Milk of Magnesia Doctor, that's all, but only recently. I've had an upset stomach and the chemist recommended it, the one in Whitby by the taxi rank. I still get the odd migraine too, not that many, but my blood pressure meant I couldn't take that stuff. Imi...'

'...gran?'

'Yeah, the prescription stuff.'

'And how much time passed, do you think, between you losing and regaining consciousness?'

'Well, seven or eight hours at least. Sometimes more. It's very unsettling.'

'SEVEN HOURS?'

'Aye... *What are you looking at me like that for?'*

Chapter Twenty-One

An Amputation at the Vet's

'Ducky duck..?'

Several miles from Doctor Waller's examination room, Maureen Moment's insubordinate tan and white terrier Bert stood stiffly to attention, hackles raised, on the slippery white examination table in the vet's at Aveyou Nympton. He was stubbornly ignoring the tatty plastic mallard, which his mother was trying to push in between his stained teeth, in an attempt to distract his attention away from the vet, who was getting himself into position in readiness to examine the agitated mongrel's back passage.

'Aww... there, there darling! Who's Mama's bwave liddle boyyy?' she cooed, trying her best not to register any sign of having heard the snarl, which had just risen menacingly in his throat.

'I think perhaps we'd all be more comfortable if you'd put his lead on and hold him tightly, Mrs Moment,' suggested the vet, 'just until we've checked him over. Otherwise, we may need to sedate him and I wouldn't want to add to your bill, just for the sake of something that may only take a few moments. It wouldn't be fair on Bert, either.'

Despite the four fingers curled snuggly around his collar, the old dog twisted around and glared at the rubber-gloved hands that were about to go where no hands had gone before.

'Sorry – he just doesn't like it when there's someone strange standing behind him,' she added apologetically. 'He gets agitated.'

'There's a good boy,' said the vet without much conviction, keeping his hands at a safe distance. Another slow snarl filled in the gap in the awkward silence.

'He's been turning round on himself for a few days now, and he keeps dragging his little bum cheeks on my carpets,' explained Maureen nervously, trying to talk down the tension in the empty room.

'Do you worm him regularly Mrs Moment?'

'Yes, just last week actually.'

'Mmmm. You say he's been eating a lot of grass in the last few days?'

'It might be because he ate a coin by accident a few days ago. It was just a small wee thing, but it worked its way out soon enough,' she said, lying easily but watching the vet's eyes for any hint of doubt.

'In that case, he'll not need an X-ray Mrs Moment, if you're sure it's come out. His lead's secure is it?'

'Yes!' She said breezily. 'It's fastened now.'

'We won't rule anything out at this stage. I suspect it could be his glands that need some attention, but if they're not the cause of his discomfort it could be some kind of parasite.'

'Goodness! I hope not!'

'Don't worry Mrs Moment. Catching a parasite isn't the worst thing that can happen to a dog. I'll be as quick as I can, a few seconds is all we need to check his glands,' he said, putting some alcohol gel onto his gloves. 'You'll have to hold him quite firmly now– ready?'

'Ready when you are, Mr Reynard.'

Bert, whose eyes were fixed on the clutch of brown spotted sausages near his hindquarters, was readying himself for the moment when they were close enough for him to make his move, although the sausages were in fact the pudgy sunburnt fingers of Mr Reynard the vet, squeezed into semi-opaque latex gloves, that were almost indistinguishable from the meaty sausages of his fantasies.

The terrible scream from the examination room took everyone in the building by surprise. So sincere and heartfelt was Dr Reynard's vocal expression of agony that his shouts caused two small girls in the waiting room to burst into tears. Laslo, a very nervous Great Dane, already on the edge of a panic attack, knocked down a display tower for *Fur and Feather* magazine then bolted for the exit, pulling his owner upright so swiftly he appeared to take flight like a water-skier snatched from a jetty. Two of the practice nurses rushed into the observation room as Maureen ran out, screaming at the receptionist to call for an ambulance as Mr Reynard chased Bert around the skirting boards, trying to retrieve his index finger from the jaws of the dastardly terrier.

'Stop that bastard dog!' roared the vet, running down the canine finger thief, as Bert streaked along the longest length of skirting towards the red leather settee.

'THE WINDOW!' yelled Maureen, realising the sash above the settee was wide open. 'BERT! NO!'

Next door to the doctor's surgery, stood the Marine Biology Research Unit and a photographic laboratory, shared by the local Technical College and Whitborough Photographic Society, who leased rooms in the building for scientific research. There was also an annexe of Leeds University's Biology department, inside which an autopsy was being conducted by a visiting Professor of Entomology, on a very unusual insect.

'Have you ever seen one of these Chris? It's a type of parasitic fly,'explained the professor to the lab technician next to him.'One of a sample the pest controller's recovered at the Gay Cavalier and the Technical College last week. Not a specimen native to the British Isles, it's safe to assume, though I haven't been able to identify the correct genus just yet. It's not in any of the reference library's source books.'

'Why's it here, in this country Prof?'

'I daresay it came over in a food container from the tropics or one of the equatorial regions– one of those destined for the supermarket depots probably. A female probably laid its eggs in some of the produce and the larvae probably hatched at some point during the journey.'

'It's very… *metallic*. Two-tone, like them trousers that mods wear.'

'Striking isn't it? If you swatted one of these it would certainly ruin your wallpaper wouldn't it? Have a look at the mouth parts under the microscope if you like… it's perfectly harmless now.'

'It's dead is it?' asked the technician, biting into an apple.

'Mmm.'

'Mmm– meaning..?'

'Mmm –meaning very probably. It hasn't shown any signs of life for some time – and it is pinned through the thorax.'

'Just a straight "yes, it's dead" will do. It's not going to come back to life if I stick my face next to it is it Prof?'

'That's highly unlikely…'

The technician leaned over the huge white microscope and grunted.

'Eurgh!.. It's got fangs on its gob!'

'I think they might be barbs for holding onto sugar cane possibly, or reeds. That's my best guess. Its physiology is quite remarkable in some respects.'

'What d'you mean?'

'It doesn't appear to have an anus.'

'No anus? A mouth – but no arse?'

'It's indicative of organisms with a short lifespan, twenty-four hours at most.'

'So they die off by themselves then?'

'Yes. Typically, these insects would have completed the biological imperatives of their life cycle in that time, then expired of natural causes, becoming a food source for other animals.'

'What kind of animal would want to eat one of these things?'

'A great range of creatures I would imagine. If they aren't consumed they'd degrade within the environment.'

'They'd rot?'

'They're not immortal. They rot down like any other creature.'

'Blumming 'eck!'

'What?'

'It's just crumbled into dust!'

'What?'

Chapter Twenty-Two

The Morning After the Night Before

Barnett had summoned the new brewery rep to assess his enthusiasm for fraud and mutual enrichment. But the man was as blind to his hints as a corpse to an alarm clock. He was starting to consider cold-blooded murder as the only possibility for relief; and was close to losing his self-control.

'Budweiser, Mr Crosbie?'

'Ahm no havin' tha shite enn heer – focken nun's pess.'

'Oh… it *is* one of the best sellers– at Victoria's and the Orange Tree. I can do it on sale or return?'

The icy glare Barnett returned, by way of an answer, made it clear any further appeals would be very unwise.

'Well, let me know if you change your mind,' mumbled the nervous rep rather uncertainly. 'Pils?'

'Fefty percent orn top o' ma reglaar order – the Becks the same. Don't thenk yee cun change ma mind sonny…y'ken?'

'Yes, of course. I…er… I… Would you like to take some Stella?'

Aye, keg an' bottled. Shame numburrs.'

'Grolsch?'

'Flash c***s drenk.'

'No Grolsch,' noted the rep, trying to keep a neutral tone, as he scribbled the last details in his order book.

'Bloodless preck...' muttered Barnett, striding off without a backwards glance.

'Mr Crosbie... I need a signature...'

'See Paula orn yer way oot. Ahm bezzy.'

Boldwood had now begun to retain some flashbacks from his nights as a supernatural being; and was beginning to record the hours lost to him. The torn clothing that was always left behind after his absences made him anxious and unsettled. It worried him that it might be found by some other person who might use it against him, in some way he couldn't yet comprehend.

He knew that he was losing control of his mind and body at certain times of the month, two or three days before and during the period around the full moon. But he had no real appreciation of the extreme nature of his affliction. In his own mind, he was simply the unlucky victim of some kind of extended blackouts or fits; not a man who transformed into a gigantic, twenty-five stone immortal eating machine, with bad breath and toothache.

After a period of contemplation and soul-searching on Tuesday afternoon, Lindsay had decided to remove himself temporarily from the hotel, on the next occasion when he felt the first symptoms of the change, the peculiar surge of energy, accompanied by a heightened sense of smell and hearing. He was already predisposed to migraines, and increasingly susceptible to episodes of constipation, in the days after his bloodthirsty forays and found it difficult to think and function in a busy environment like the Shirestones, whilst suffering the cumulative effects of his various conditions, though his blood pressure at least was no longer a problem.

His main priority was to avoid putting himself in a position where someone else might witness one of his maniacal rages or catch him semi-naked in the afterglow of his unconscious fits. He wished to avoid being an object of ridicule, but what really preyed on his mind was the risk of being taken away from his beloved hotel and locked up in an institution – it was this he wanted to avoid at all costs.

To this end, he had decided to use the lease he'd been offered on a static caravan, on a small site above Runswick Bay, as a bolthole during his next cluster of seizures. The owner of the land, one of his business partners, lived in a small bungalow at the extreme edge of an adjacent plot and rarely ventured out, having lost both his legs as a child due to complications arising from a polio infection. His sister, a nurse at Whitby Hospital was his only regular visitor. It was an ideal situation for Lindsay, which almost guaranteed his privacy. There were only two more caravans on hard standings, separated by trees nearby, and the field itself was surrounded by a thick hedge. It offered him a perfect place to hide out and was far enough away from Cloughton to protect his anonymity.

Back in Whitborough's old town, Barnett was treating a whisky-induced headache with great gulps of dark brown tea and hiding behind his Torremolinos gangster shades, on a stool by the downstairs bar of Mystery City, punching the keys of his desk calculator with an old commando dagger. James Stone emerged from behind the stage with a plastic coffee cup full of coins.

'Collecten' Jamesy?'

'Aye Barn, sexteen quedd frum the floors… yersell?'

'C★★t frum the brewery… we have nae seen eye tae eye yet.'

'Thenk yull tunn th' wee squitt?'

'Oh aye. Either that or the c★★t's gann swemmen off th' bay enn concrete socks. Hoo's warr Brandon's heed, by the way? Dedd we really have a focken donkey enn the utility?'

'Sheemsho… great pile o' horseshite orn the flooer. Focken students probably. Brandon's sound – a few wee stetches.'

'Rag week prank eh? Funny theng tho' thuzz a wee smeyll o' gas enn the annexe Barn.'

'Gas ya say? The inlet pipe's enn there no?'

'Aye. Looks okay tae mee. Ah cannae see a crack. No chance of a belddup, wi'all the grille vents anyways.'

'Know hoo they check gas pipe seals enn the trawlers Jamesy? Dilute Fairy lequedd. Whart they dae, ezz wet the wee pipe yee want tae check see, eff the pipe seals blaze bubbles – yuv gort a leak?' Ma nephews learnt me that…'

'That's focken clever… I'll go check masell wee shome enn a mennett.'

'Leave yerr smokes enside the now. Ah dinnae want another mess tae clean up, yer soft c★★t. Hoo many bogs blocked?'

'Two enn' the men's, three in the hens'. Don the Rod's cummen tae vac 'em oot.'

At Beautimann Buerk and Trippe's offices, Derek was starting to flag, and was having to hold himself together after lunch until their doors finally shut at 4.30. He was the only partner in the firm to vote against their yearly 'open door day', arguing it demeaned their profession and was ultimately counter-productive. But he had been outvoted and was forced to engage in a tradition which he disdained. Fortunately, it was agreed that each partner was allowed to drop a day every second year, though this privilege was not extended to their legal secretaries. Derek had just finished advising a young man, on his intention to recover costs for works carried out on behalf of the prospective buyer for his house, who had pulled out of the sale, just before the exchange of contracts, when he heard the voice of Isla Binnie in reception.

'Hiya Maureen, ah want tae speak tae Derek.'

'Oh! He's with a client at the moment Isla,' explained Maureen, stiffly.

'That's alreet, I'll jusht park masell orn the wee bench here hen,' she said, going to the waiting area by the front window.

'I'm not sure how long he'll be Isla. We do close at 4.30 today.'

'Aye hen. Ah know tha'. Ten mennetts ez all ah need.'

Chapter Twenty-Three

Curry Night

Inspector Marshall and Detective Sergeant Broadhead met at the front doors of the popular Eastern Spice Indian restaurant at the corner of Market Square and Pastry Lane for their weekly curry binge. Arriving from opposite directions, they nodded discreetly to each other then walked inside into the lounge and reception area, making their way to the front desk to exchange a few words with their host, Anil 'Paddy' Khurmi – nicknamed 'Paddy' after his love of Guinness and whisky– and to speak to his brothers, Prince, Aadi and Aarif.

'Evening Anil. We'll have a couple of pints of Kingfisher to start us off.'

'Good evening Raymond, George, how are you – nice night?'

'We'd be much less well if we had to miss your grub, Anil. Always a pleasure.'

'Pleasure is ours also, always. We have new beer, very tasty. Is old in India, but new for us – Kalyani, nice flavour, but bottles only.'

'Thanks Paddy, but we'll stick with the usual for now.'

'You like to try? No charge? With Kingfisher…'

'What d'you say George. Shall we try some?'

'Very kind. Aye. I'm game.'

'I chill two bottles– send you cold?'

'Well, it's not every day we get an offer like that.'

'Ahh good. All well. I bring menus…'

'Give us twenty minutes will you Anil. Don't keep anyone else waiting on our account. We're just going to have a chat between ourselves.'

'Ahh is work. I hope is not us you put in cell!'

'I make a point never to upset the people who cook my food Anil. Can we have a pickle tray and six poppadoms– before the menus – I'm not sure about George, but I'm famished. I might even have enough space left for a dessert tonight.'

'I'm a tad that way meself– I could eat the bloody arm on your sofa Anny,' added George jokingly, eyeballing the enormous leather suite in front of the windows.

'Ahh excellent, but no coffee ice-cream. Smaller freezer is leak. We have table for you as always by window, follow me please.'

'New member of staff?' asked Marshall, catching sight of one of the waiters dashing past.

'Only part-time – start tonight.'

'He looks vaguely familiar… What's his name?'

'Cubitt. He is cousin Ray.'

'Cubitt– the palmist?'

'He is not in kitchen. Front of house only,' added Anil's brother, hurriedly.

'He's serving food?'

'He needs work, we need help.'

'He's serving food? Not reading palms?'

'No. No palms. Drinks and food. He had no work, since big ship stink. Boom! Boom! He say Anil, I no see catastrophe,

164

cannot look customer in eye, people ask me. He say – I put away – spirit things. Art of fortune calling.'

'Well…'

Once the two policemen were alone, they began to relax and talk about the less attractive aspects of life in the police service and the many shortcomings of their colleagues.

'Despite what some of those twerps at the station may think, I'm not *enjoying* my suspension, or whatever d'Ascoyne wants to call it George, but I am making the most of it,' emphasised Inspector Marshall thoughtfully, though a playful smirk settled into the lines of his face.

'Our d'Ascoyne is having second thoughts – about kicking you out on sick leave I think. He doesn't like being on the spot, having his door rapped on every few minutes. I get the feeling he's a little intimidated by this crew from MI5 and the Home Office. Are you going to see someone from the Union?'

'Certainly not. I want some leverage when the time's right, so I'm keeping a low profile. If I make a complaint I'll never get back in where I want to be, that lot will just close ranks and everything will turn to shit. I want a nice, quiet, low-profile return. Slowly, slowly catchee monkey – isn't that what Fu keeps saying?'

'You're not as daft as you look, are you guv?'

'I hope the chief's respecting my office is he? I don't want to come back to someone else's mess. I know my desk isn't the best kept workspace in the building, but I do know where everything is and where I like it.'

'Don't worry. It's still locked. Did you need anything from the f-cabs?'

'There's a book I'd quite like George, one of those that I

borrowed from the reference library. It's in the second drawer under my desk.'

'I'll try my best guv.'

'It's a big hardback, *The History of the Luftwaffe 1933-45*; it's under my ashtray. If there's no one looking, could you empty it in the bin in the corridor outside? I left a bit of me sandwich in it, and it's probably past its best by now. I need the old Hooper files copying too – do you think you can manage it?'

'In the grey f-cab?'

'Aye, the taller one. The historical crimes section. It'll be near the back, everything from 1940-65.'

'That's gonna keep the copier busy for a while. I'll have to stand next to it while it's spewing them out to keep the nosy parkers away.'

'I'm sure you'll cope. Just give 'em your best look.'

'What if the Super pokes his head round the door?'

'Tell the nosy sod you're running off some copies of the Federation newsletter, that'll make him scarper. After we're finished scoffing here I need you to see something I've been working on at home, so we'll order a taxi before we settle up. I'm sure you'll find it interesting George.'

'Deighton's applied for CID – in the Met.'

'Has he by jove?'

'You don't seem surprised.'

'No, I'm not. Our little service is but a stepping stone,' said Marshall, mockingly, taking up a stiff-backed, Quasimodo-like posture in jest.

'Mmm, that's nice,' added Marshall, savouring a mouthful of beer. 'D'you think he'll hack it?'

'Well, they've got as many bent 'uns and lazy bastards as

the West Yorkshire force. Who knows? If he finds a father figure like our Sergeant Dodds to hide behind he might be all right. If he's unlucky, I'd say six months – tops,' said Broadhead, taking a long draught of Kalyani.'That is nice. Strong stuff... I think I'll stick with the Kingfisher with the food though.'

'My thoughts exactly. You need something clean and neutral with Indian or Thai food, I find. Helps to get to grips with the spices without overwhelming the taste buds. You couldn't have a craft beer with this kind of food.'

'Too right. Old Peculier, or– God forbid – Pebbletrees Old Bob, we'd be on the Alka-Seltzer all night.'

'I wonder if that business at the Keys wasn't down to too much drink, and our Mr Austin's famous temperament,' said Marshall, thinking aloud.

'If you'd put that lot in any pub in town I doubt it would have been very different. Just think what could have happened if they'd gone into the Fleur de Lys, or the Drummer Boy; it would have been a massacre,' added Broadhead, dropping the names of two popular Irish pubs, whose clientele were known for their strong Republican sympathies.

'Well, that was the verdict anyway, wasn't it? According to the esteemed editor of the *Whitborough Gazette*. The Milk Race Massacre– the tabloid copywriters are missing a kindred spirit aren't they.' Do you know anyone in those pubs – personally I mean?'

'The Fleur de Lys and the Boy? You must be joking guv. Did you ask for a pickle tray?'

'Yeah. But they're making us some fresh dips. Perks of the job. No eastern Europeans?'

'No. Never been in. Bad luck those cyclists turning up

when they did. But it's their fault as much as the Navy, they were going way too fast round that bend. They could have bloody killed somebody.'

'Well they got their comeuppance. The tape is quite a hit, I've heard?'

'That's one way of putting it, I asked Elland to make a few extra copies,' continued Broadhead, 'on top of the statutories for evidence – with Mr Candy's permission, of course,' he said, winking.'I took one down to Des Brownlee at the Rugby Club. They're playing it as a pre-match treat for the first team.'

'A pre-match treat? God almighty! That'll get their blood up.'

'So George, what'll you have? I'm going to go for lamb skewers and Afghani chicken again, lemon rice with an okra bhaji and chickpea paneer.'

'Are we sharing a taxi to your house?'

'Are you casting aspersions on my digestive system?'

'For the record boss, your arse stinks, but so does mine – *ooof,*' said Broadhead, gurning, shifting his cheek.

'Can't you do that somewhere else?' hissed Marshall. 'Wave your bloody napkin!'

'I can't do that, they'll know what I've done…'

'Oh – *so it's all right to do it in my company is it George* – thank *you* very much.'

'Sorry. I didn't think you'd mind…'

'Bloody charming…'

After their meal, and another round of drinks, the two men decided to order their taxi for the short drive to Inspector Marshall's house on Leather Lane. Marshall made them both a mug of tea, then led the way upstairs to the main bedroom in his 1940's semi which now functioned as an office and study, since his wife's illness had forced her to live with her sister, closer to the hospital.

'Take a seat George, just move the files off whichever chair takes you fancy. D'you want a Castella?'

'That'd be nice. Where's this thing you wanted to show me?'

'It's in a leather cover. In that box file… in the middle of the desk. I'll be back in a second,' said Marshall, descending the stairs to retrieve his box of cigars. Broadhead lifted the lid on the box file, and began to read…

Below, is the full text of a covering letter, sewn to the front of an aged nappa document jacket, protecting a sheaf of old papers. The letter was written in copperplate script, in loose hand, by Doctor Bartholomew Broadhead –a Whitborough man, in the early years of the last century. It was deposited, with the aforementioned documents late one evening at the reception counter within the foyer of Whitborough police station, at around midnight on the 31st of March 1983, by persons unknown. No letters of introduction, or accompanying notes, pertaining to its anonymous keeper(s) were found with the contents.

The following record is the outcome of many days and nights of careful study, into papers wych came into my possession by chance, through the administration of an inheritance. The elderly document file we have recovered, in wych the papers were found, consists of many transcripts, declarations and statements, together with a comprehensive collection of dockets, receipts and invoices – all of wych are in a goodly state–butt furnish a riddle.

They would undoubtedly have remained undiscovered and hydden from the worlde for many more years, or possibly forever –were it not for a sudden resolution between my brother, Samuel Gerald Broadhead and I, to inspect the roomes of an old propertie, previously unknown to us. A propertie that has recently passed into the temporary guardianship of oure family's solicitor, Mr Eldred Garvey of Long Acre. It is to oure advantage, that the propertie in question is also situated on the same street as oure own Mr Garvey. The building owned by the late Mr Clout, and all that remains within, will eventually be sold, to satisfy the requirements of the will in question.

My brother Samuel and I were the first of oure kin to apply for permission to view the building, and the first to obtain the keys that Friday afternoon. We were allowed four houres by Mr Garvey and set out to find the building without any notion of what we might discover therein. Long Acre, is best described as Whytborough's Royal Mile and lies upon the olde processional way to the headland used by the Druids, the Anglo Saxons and the Romans in early times. It is not the equal in length, of that famous avenue in a certain Scottish city, to wych I allude, but is its equal in width. The central ribbon of the carriageway is usefully paved with large flagstones, edged with two contrasting courses of flat faced granite bricks –laid to a Flemish bond pattern –abutting the recessed concave guttering stones. The pavements are also generously broad and of the same good quality.

It is an uncommon privilege, to be able to inspect the home of a deceased stranger to whoome one suddenly finds oneself related. As the late Mr Clout was unfamiliar to us –and we to him, from birth until death, oure visit to his former dwelling place was not the sad inspection it might have been; rather, it was a happy affair and an opportunity for discovery, the only valid emotion one can give into under such circumstances, is a feeling of regret –for it is not healthy to dwell on lost opportunities to make acquaintances and relations such as we have missed in ignorance. One must practice equanimity in the face of all the twists and turns in life that fate and fortune can bestow. It was in this spirit, that we arrived at the propertie and began oure perusal.

Long Acre is comprised of six separate blocks of towne houses, three are very olde, the last in line are of equal length, butt of the modern era and furthermost from the castle keep. All ascend to three storeys, though the smooth faced modern terraces built in the reign of King George are very much higher, having high ceilings and tall broad windows, replicating the classical proportions of Romano-Grecian proportions. All enjoy a fine view over Victoria Bay and the red tiled roofes of the olde town, beyond the wide lawns and time worn headstones of St Mary's Cemetery.

Number Seven, the home of the recently deceased Mr Clout, is part of the older run of buildings and follows the pattern begun by the first built pair of adjoining houses, wych are all accessed by a flight of steps from the pavement. The lower part of the terrace is made of block stone, some being of massive size (undoubtedly rubble stone from the castle's former structures) whilst the upper storeys are the best example of the cage and infill tradition in the towne. We were pleased to discover, a rich interior – finely kept, with many artefacts and souvenirs from the far lands of the known worlde. It was whilst I was backing up to better observe one of his curiosities, that I accidentally breached one of the plaster and lath infill panels with the press of my rump. Once I had dusted myself down and had suffered the ridicule of my sibling, we inspected the breach. It was there, beneath the cracked plaster where we discovered the file in question. In an aperture hacked out of the lath and horsehair infill, wych had been repaired with a scratch coat of plaster and then thinly skimmed to complete its concealment.

Whether Mr Clout knew of its existence we shall know not, butt as one of the benefactors of his estate, it is not –I should suppose, improper for me to retain them temporarily for study. As the most learned and able son of the family in matters of commerce, writing and contracts.

The documents and records, found there, cover the whole period of the trial of seven local men from the borough of Whytborough and contain the compleat sworn testimonies of three defendants, the record of the clerk of the court, two drafts of a speech made by the foreman of the jury and the written record of the summing up by the judge. Together with the aforementioned dockets. The papers are quite olde, butt are otherwise in excellent condition. Most importantly, they enable a comprehensive and fulsome understanding of events from the many perspectives represented therein. I am of the opinion, that it is likely they have never been examined since they were bound and sealed inside theire satchel upon the dismissal of the jury and the closure of the case. The infill recess, in wych they were deposited, has undoubtedly aided the preservation of its contents. The house itself is contemporary with the events detailed in the file.

The trial was conducted in the autumn of 1645, after the

172

surrender of the garrison of Whytborough Castle. Though the events described bridge the period before and after the surrender. The purpose of these proceedings, seems to have been to decide the fate of two bands of brigands, and theire failed attempt to apprehend a Royalist breakout, independent of the official Parliamentary forces. Theire enterprise seems to have been frown'd upon as much for its secrecy as its calamitous conclusion, in the shadow of the death of a priest "by visitation of a wilde beast, or hell hound." For nothing was recovered by either of the partees. Rascal adventurers in the mould of Raleigh, even in the bloom of success, are now rarely in favour in oure time, unlucky adventurers even less so. It seems the same mood influenced the conduct of the the judge and jury during the proceedings.

The assembly of the jury itself, also seems to have been conducted under an atmosphere of bad faith. All butt one of theire number –a Merchant named Troy, were press ganged with some resentment, from the reluctant ranks of commoners. An ill received speech by a seer and fortune teller, one Ethel Penrose broke up the first –she is recorded as being imprison'd in the toll bar for the duration. Though paradoxically the public benches were neare to collapse under the weight of theire audience.

It is clear, (even from a cursory study of the record) that the real purpose for its conduct was twofold: to put into the public domain, knowledge that might encourage suitable persons to institute a search, to recover the Treasure wych at that juncture was assumed lost. Finally, to inflict a punishment sufficient enough to deter any searches and enquiries outside the jurisdiction of the Alderman's office.

It should be noted that certain final testimonies admitted

by the defendants contain a supernatural element. In addition, there were irregular but significant references in the court documents to an unusual miasma about the building during the days the trial was held and strange weather effects within. Unusually cold temperatures were recorded that compelled the assembly to remain swaddled in theire hattes and cloakes and comforters. In spite of this, all the public pews were taken –as stated in my previous paragraph, and there seems to have been some competition to get within earshot of the Bench. Within the body of invoices, are delivery notes for extra candles and coal for the brazier and stove. These appear to be in addition to theire fixed purchases. *(Note –it must have been a remarkably bitter autumn.)* Last amongst these is a request for payment, 'for oure aforementioned preparatory works, ministries, ceremonies and blessings, conducted by J.B.L., *(EXCST) R.C.C* rendered to the building and congregation' from the Bishopric. *(Note –this document has caused me great difficulties, in my enquiries, why is its wording so deliberately obscure. Who was J.B.L. What title or occupation is given for this gentleman? For he was undoubtedly a man of rank or position in the Roman Catholic faith or a person of note, worthy of a degree of deference.)*

Alas, there is no building still extant, such as that wych was described for the trial within the borough. I have begun investigations to determine its former setting, though I have only discovered a brief reference to a fire, attributed to a lightning storm in the year 1646 in the part of the old town, where I suspect the court house may have stood. There are a handful of empty plots left now in places that may have favoured a building of its size or any ruine, prodigiously decayed that may be identified as such.

(At this point the formal record ends and the thread

continues in rough note form, on the rear of a theatre bill poster. Presumably, to conserve the recorder's own stock of paper.)

I shall not set down my quill just yet, so early in my investigation. As newes has come to me from several sources in the towne, of persons who may be willing to add to my knowledge of this curious business. This afternoon I am to visit a goode friend of a relative of the trial judge, who may yet be able to shed light on this episode.

A final paragraph was hurriedly appended as a footnote to this soon afterward.

In my haste to examine these old documents, I had failed to inspect properly, theire leather coverlet. The sheath is unremarkable at first sight –I had foolishly assumed, it was unworthy of examination until I had cause to seize it up to avoid staining the hide by my clumsiness. There is a small deerskin pocket behind the front containing a gold coin, wrapped in a scrap of parchment. More peculiar still, a strange diagram containing obscure symbols appeared upon the paper –when I had the opportunity to examine it in the light of my window. It was not rendered with any great skill, but was, I imagine, perfectly adequate for its purpose, which I surmise is connected with some occult ritual. The illustration, a line drawing without perspective or shadow, appears thus –a large square encloses a second smaller square –tilted ninety degrees from the vertical, forming the outline of a diamond within. Inside the diamond lies another square in the same positional aspect as the first, enclosing a circle; inside this, lies another circle divided into foure quarters. Each segment contains a word, a symbol, or a letter. I have identified some symbols from an olde paper on astrological symbolism, given to me by my housemaster at Brasenose (a college of Oxford University) many years ago. There is a glyph representing the planet Mars, the Moon and Sun and letters from the Torah. I have decided to take this to my appointment. The sky has become very dark suddenly, so my brother and I have summoned a gig. We should not like to arrive at the house of oure host with new hattes and breeches spotted by rain.

In my own hand,

Doctor of Medicine, Bartholomew Broadhead 11th November, 1815.

'Is this it?'

'I think so.'

'Nothing else?'

'No. Dropped off at the front desk when Moyne had his back turned. Somehow, it's made its way onto mine.'

'What's the CCTV shown up, sir?'

'You can see for yourself tomorrow. It's in old Barry's grotto,' said Inspector Marshall slowly, name-checking the sergeant in charge of the records and evidence room in the bowels of the station.

'But– you've seen it?'

'I have George. There's something bloody strange about it, though Barry says he checked it and couldn't find any damage or faults in the tape or the tracking. I can't say I'm that keen on watching it again. Why don't you have a look at it?'

'What d'you mean when you say there's something not right about it?'

'Whoever dropped those papers off had a strange effect, on the recording.'

'Strange effect on the recording?'

Inspector Marshall shifted in his seat and looked out of the window, looking as if he would rather be somewhere else, then pressed his fist into the fold of skin underneath his chin, stroking his emerging whiskers.

'Everything around this *mystery visitor* on our tape is clear, but the figure itself is just a blurry, featureless shadow – the way it moves gives me the creeps. He's copied it and sent the first tape to one of our labs for tests. *Outside of the norm…'* mumbled Marshall, shifting his shoulders, as if he was trying to shrug off the cold touch of an invisible hand.

'I seem to remember hearing you saying that before,' said Broadhead, attempting a smile – as an antidote to offset to his boss's sour grimace.

'You wouldn't be going to bed with a smirk like that if you'd watched it,' said Marshall slowly, with a very serious expression, 'but let's forget about it for now. I've been through the rest of those papers twice, and there's nothing more after that date in November. Except for this,' he said, handing over a photocopy of an old document, with a serious air. 'It's Dr Bartholomew Broadhead's death certificate. This Doctor Broadhead chap was killed on the same day he wrote that last paragraph on the covering letter – November the eleventh. The cause of death is recorded as crushing blow to the head, by a loose stone corbel that fell from the pediment of the Vicarage of St Mary's, on Long Acre.'

'Pediment?'

'It's a stone porch. An overhang. Like the one at the front of the market hall.'

'Poor bugger. What's a corbel?'

'They look like carved bookends George, turned upside

down; they're like a support, they're not small things– if one of those hit you you'd be dead before you hit the ground. Do you think he could have been a relation of yours? How many Broadheads are there in Whitborough?'

'I suppose it's possible. To be quite honest, I don't know how long our family's been around these parts. I know we've been around at least a hundred and fifty years. I suppose I *could* find out. Do I need to find out?'

'It might be useful, I don't know yet. Don't go out of your way just at the moment. Just make some discreet enquiries – inside the family if you like. That should be enough for now.'

'So how is this crap old stack of paperwork relevant, to your, er… *our* situation?'

'The advantage of being *persona non grata*, is the amount of spare time I have to really look into things. All the crazy goings on here recently. And one word keeps cropping up again and again – GOLD,' said Marshall, making an exaggerated 'O' shape with his mouth, as he stretched out the second letter.

'Gold. Here in Whitborough… I'll be damned… is this connected to that throwaway comment you made to Beautimann before we went into his office?'

'Yes George, it is. Do you recall his reaction?' said Marshall, smiling. 'I should add, the gold coin mentioned in this chap's notes was in the pouch mentioned in the covering letter with those scraps of paper.'

'You're kidding…'

'Most of the information I've managed to gather suggests it was a large hoard of gold coins and some jewels too. It was originally kept in a single chest and then split into smaller boxes, before it was moved. That would make sense, but no one I've spoken to thinks it ever left the district. All the people

I've spoken to are convinced it was hidden around here, hundreds of years ago. This isn't just hearsay – it's historical fact. It disappeared at the end of the siege at the castle during the English Civil War. What if some gang has found it after all this time? Then had a falling out. People do stupid things for money. Reckless things. *Dangerous* things. This trial was a sham, reading between the lines, a reckoning after the fact. A fortune went missing out from under the noses of the New Model Army and their bosses in London – and they were angry.'

'But how can anyone really be sure it's still in the area… after all this time?'

'Well, gold – like anything valuable – leaves a trail doesn't it? It's very hard for anyone to explain the sudden arrival of conspicuous wealth without any apparent means. Tongues wag, people become greedy and jealous and before long you've got murder and corpses, OR CRIMES OF VIOLENCE. *And what a lot of that we've had, all of a sudden.*'

'Mmm. What do you make of the references – or inferences to that supernatural stuff?'

'I wouldn't give too much credence to it. I think it's a load of old codswallop,' said Marshall without much vim.

'Made up to scare people off?'

'That's what I'd say. It would have been an effective tactic to put off the more nervous and superstitious crooks. I don't think it would have stopped them all. You can never do that. But the theory is sound enough; I dare say it would work now too, to an extent.'

'Who did you get this information from?'

'Well, funnily enough, the wife's sister is married to a one of the history teachers at the sixth form. He's a member of that historical society– the Sealed Knot. The ones that get pissed on mead and charge around castles and fields, clubbing each other with blunt poleaxes. Only Colin doesn't do any of the rough stuff anymore, since Oliver Cromwell's shire horse kicked him in the ging gang goolies. I went for a drink in the Stage Door with him a few nights ago to pick his brains. He's what you might call an English Civil War expert. Filled me in on the siege here and the legend of the Treasure of the Mar del Norte.'

'Mar del Norte?'

'It's Spanish for "the Treasure of the Northern Sea", the North Sea in other words.'

'Only you and I know about this piece of gold though. That's the way I want it to stay for now. I'd like to find out a bit more about the coin.'

'Is that slippery old queen Chipping still at the museum?'

'Yes, he is. I'm sure our paths will cross again in the near future,' said Marshall very slowly and seriously. There's a coin expert at York University I'm going to see tomorrow – though he doesn't know it yet. While I'm freelance I'm going to make the most of it. Just to keep you in the loop, there's a third party involved. I can't prove it yet, but I'm working on it…'

Chapter Twenty-Four

The Forum

PUBLIC NOTICE
ALL RESIDENTS OF KETTLENESS & RUNSWICK BAY.

Invitation to attend a meeting of local landowners & residents

Bethel Methodist Chapel, Lazy-Jane Lane.
7pm Tuesday

Chair *Mr C. Thatcher* **Guest Speakers** *PC J.Alger Lady Warner Woollens & Ibrahim Kinte of Charlwood Estate and Zoo.*

Tea and coffee. No children/pets. Free parking for the duration in the chapel car park. **No tractors/horses/quadbikes.**

The chapel was full to capacity, even before PC Alger arrived in his white Ford Escort, straddling the road and the verge because there were no spaces left inside the chapel yard. Inside the chapel, the congregation was already in discussion amongst themselves, locked into a dozen private huddles.

'Wharrabout yoo – ave yoo lost owt Arthur?'

'Ahv not lost nowt. Us dogs 'ull tell us if there's strangers abaht,' replied Arthur Garbutt, owner of Hilltop Bungalow.

'Well, tha's nay got n' livestock now anyroad. Nowt 'cept yer 'ens,' added Albie Gall, one pew behind.

'Ahm telling y'all, summat's bin tekkin' us ewes. Uz lost two ram an' all this week,' announced Wilf Thatcher, the younger brother of Conn Thatcher, owner of Harker Farm and the largest acreage in the district, talking to a small crowd of his peers, a few benches away from Arthur and Albie.

'Likely as not, bugger's smelt a yew in't next valley, an' got jumped by a dog,' muttered Albie, earwigging on the group of younger men.

'It's a strange dog that leaves a ram wi'out its guts an' its face on, Mr Gall,' replied Wilf, hearing the interruption.

'Mebbee we've got one o' them big cats. Paper sez some lass from Burniston saw one tekkin' a drink in Scalby Beck when she were out wi' 'er dogs. That musta given 'em a bloody fright.'

'Ahm not convinced it's right for 'em round 'ere. There's probably a few down int south west, granted. But not up 'ere. Too bloody cold. They'd be nithered,' said Arthur.

'Nothing that's native to this country could leave our ram looking like it did. Unless we've got a fox the size of a Great Dane in Kettleness. One things fo' sure, it weren't suicide,' added Wilf.

'Thee 'Ound of Death,' said Jack Farrar of Midstream Cottage suddenly, under his breath.

'Yer what?' snapped Arthur.

'Thee 'Ound of Death,' said Jack again– quite seriously, wearing his best miserable face.

'Thee 'Ound o' Death! I never heard such a load o' bloody nonsense,' groaned Sandy Talbot, the most vocal appointee of the Neighbourhood Watch committee. 'Some discussion this is turning out to be. Where's Jackson?'

'Out front talking ta Conn. Reckon they're wondering where that Lady Woollens woman is.'

'Bloody gentry's alluz late. It's only us bloody low-born fools that shows up on time.'

'Is everyone here? asked PC Alger, stopping in front of Conn Thatcher and his other brother Jim, who were smoking grubby roll-ups on the top step just beyond the small chapel's front door.

'Aye. Everyone oos anyone an' t'rest that wants ta be somebody– eh Jim?'

'Appen yer reet.'

'You're a way from home, Jim. What brings you up here?' asked Alger, surprised to see Conn Thatcher's second brother.

'This an'that. Not much going on in Thornton Dale, the odd duck rape, about as excitin' as it gets for us. I thought I'd get me sen ovver 'ere fo' some excitement. That an' me mam's birthday party the neet.'

'Well, wish her well, from me an' Jenn.'

'Aye. I will. Thanks Jackson. So what's the crack? Funny business round 'ere I 'ear.'

'Hard to say Jim. We thought we might have a bit of rustling and some nutcase that likes disfiguring livestock, but it's gone beyond that. I've organised this so we can all get together and see what we can come up with between us. It's just a forum really, but maybe I'll find out something I didn't know before.'

'Well, reckon it's what we need. Nice to see us neighbours– whatever. Most of 'em...' Time for us ta gan in then. Let's be 'aving yer…' said Conn to Jim and Jackson, ushering the younger men inside.

Once Conn Thatcher had announced the start, at the lectern, and explained the format and timetable, he introduced Jackson to the hall and then sat at the front, facing his neighbours with Wilf and Don Wilkin, the beach warden.

'Well, thank you all for coming,' said PC Alger from the front of the small fiddlers' stage at the back of the chapel… 'it's good to see such a big turnout so late on a Sunday. You all know why we're here. Can I start by asking if anyone here has any fresh evidence or theories concerning these thefts and disappearances?'

'Thefts, is it?' muttered Jack derisively under his cap, keeping his eyes on the bible rail of the pew, far below the sight line of his companions and friends.

'Do you have anything you want to share with us Jack?' asked Jackson, hearing something from the older man, but not hearing the exact words of his contribution as he mumbled at the back of his pew.

'Jack thinks it's summat other than that, that us simple folks think it might be, eh Jack?' said Albie, managing to be sarcastic, obscure and diplomatically vague all at once.

'I've said me piece,' replied Jack, cutting off his neighbour's smirk with a loveless glare.

'I was told the zoo were going to send their manager here to speak to us,' shouted Mrs Halshaw from the back. 'Or Lady Woollens…'

'They were Mrs Halshaw, but they're now certain that nothing in the park has escaped,' explained the constable, emolliently.

'Well I would have expected some sort of recognition from them; that park is full of dangerous wild animals after all. It would have been polite of them to send somebody, if only to show some solidarity or some curiosity,' she said, by way of a grumble.

'That zoo was one of our first destinations Mrs Halshaw, but we no longer have any reason to continue with that particular line of enquiry. I don't think it's necessary or desirable for them to be here, now we've ruled out the possibility that one of their animals escaped.'

Jack Farrar put both of his enormous gnarled hands on the top rail of the pew in front of him and stood up slowly, supporting himself, then sighed heavily and looked left to right, still unwilling to greet the eyes of his neighbours with any warmth, not through shyness, as he was not a nervous person by anyone's definition of the word, or someone with anything to hide. He had spent his working years looking at the soil and the skies and all of God's creatures above and beneath, but he still hadn't found another human being who hadn't disappointed him in some way. Jack cleared his throat and waited for the rest of the congregation to fall silent before offering his parting contribution to the hall.

'Yuv all lost livestock. Two campers is missin' and Mr and Mrs 'alshaws cat. Consecutive neets. An' what time were it in yer almanacs? But folk won't see what they can't or won't. I've said all I'm gonna say an' I'll not say no more now. I'll be on me way.'

Without another word, he touched his flat cap and ambled out of the chapel without a backward glance, raising a couple of meaty fingers as a parting gesture to Constable Alger, who was not comforted by his sudden decision to leave, though he made no attempt to encourage him to stay, partly because he was slightly intimidated by the old farmer and partly because he was trying to read the rest of his audience to try and identify any other potential deserters.

'One down,' commented Arthur, drily.

'What did he say about almanacs, Dad?' said Wilf, licking the seam of another rolly.

'Time o'day worrit– or summat?' said one of the other men present.

'If there is anything you haven't mentioned already, either to me or each other about this business it would be really useful for us all to hear it now. It might even connect with what we know already and give us all a clearer picture of what we're dealing with…' continued the constable; we can rule out escaped animals from the zoo, and the livestock thieves from Grassingtown as they're in custody.'

'Has anyone looked in the sea caves?' asked Councillor Halshaw. 'There's quite a few on our stretch. Near Seaforth.'

'Near Meredith's place?'

'Aye, below Meredith's place.'

'Why don't we get some people together and some torches and see what we can find?'

'An excellent idea Councillor. Do we have any volunteers?' asked the constable.

Twelve hands were raised, though Alger barely held half the room.

'I'll come if your lot can rustle up some torches,' said Albie – then groaned as his wife elbowed him sharply in the ribs. 'If I can't find me own, that is,' he muttered.

'That's better – you tight old bugger…' said Albie's wife.

'I'm sure I can persuade our stores to issue anyone who

wants to help with torches and whistles,' announced Alger drily.

'Be useful if yer can get some 'o them reflective coats 'an all. An' a pile of 'ard 'ats Jackson. Some 'o them caves go back a ways,' added Conn. 'It'll 'ave to be a Saturday, certainly for us and most of the other folk hereabouts I reckon.'

'Who will come and help us search if I can get you all the right equipment?' asked the constable again. 'Can we have another show of hands? We'll go with Conn's suggestion for Saturday, this Saturday at noon everyone?'

This time, except for Mrs Halshaw – who was completely the wrong shape for anything more challenging than a theme park grotto – Alger had won the room.

'Has anyone checked Standard Copse and the old jet mine yet?' asked Mr Halshaw?'

'A good suggestion Councillor. I've arranged for a group of police cadets from Northallerton to sweep it on Friday afternoon. Some rangers from the North Yorkshire Parks Authority are going to look inside the mine on Sunday. Does anyone have any other information or suggestions?'

Jack Farrar was still sitting on the lifeboat memorial bench, on the opposite side of the road to the chapel when the meeting finally broke up and the crowd made their way to their cars and Land Rovers. Jack was smoking his pipe, enigmatically; watching the rainwater trails from the fields twist down the steep strip of faded tarmac that was Lazy-Jane Lane into the Kettleness cauldron.

Conn Thatcher, seeing Jack sitting alone, wandered over the road and sat down on the bench beside him, taking out his own pipe briefly, returning it to the frayed top pocket of his green gilet after tapping out the ash.

'Can I give yer a lift 'ome Jack? I've got ta drop some feed off at mine before I go past yours, but the lads have got their trucks, if you'd rather go wi' them.'

'Aye very kind Conn, I'll go with thee if that's alreet. Be nice to see the farm.'

'What about this business then Jack? What d'ya mek of it?'

'I'll not say, I don't think– in front o' them that's inside. Just make sure yer bairns are inside of a night, and the lambs. Then's the danger.'

'Jack, we've known each other forty year. Yer can say owt in front o' me. I'm not gonna share a confidence wi'no one.'

'You'll not thank me for telling yer old friend. And the worst of it is, once ya know what I found, you'll have nay choice but to keep it to y'sen. Just like me, festering away,' he said tapping his fist against his chest. I thought we might be one of the lucky generations it passes by. There's no stopping what can't be stopped, ay. It'll be tough on some of us.'

'What are you talking about Jack? You're not mekking a right lot of sense, if you don't mind me saying.'

'You need to get to St Hilda's in Whitby and see it for yerself. The Whitefield's and the Comery's family records boxes. They're kept on the vestry bookcase. Reverend's out Friday afternoons, but he don't lock the door. It's a moss green leather box, tatty black cotton lining. Give yer sen a couple of hours. Then mek yer own judgement. It's wrapped up wi' our families anyway. And the Comerys in Robin 'oods Bay. I think I'll walk home now, actually Conn,' said Jack, preparing to stand again. 'I've a mind to be alone if you'll forgive me. Just mek sure yer go to the vestry on yer own. When you've seen it, come an' see me.'

Only minutes after Jack Farrar got back home to Midstream Cottage, he realised he had a visitor, in the shape of the community policeman, standing nervously by his back door.

'Jackson is it?'

'Yes Mr Farrar, sorry to surprise you – so soon after the meeting. May I come in for a minute or two?'

'Reckon so… you took yer time lad, but I'll not say you're not welcome. Thought you'd be round, didn't we Ned?' said the old farmer, patting the head of his Staffordshire Bull Terrier, who was trying to stuff a felt reindeer into Jackson's crotch.'Eee must like yer lad. Only shows Rudolph to 'iz best pals. Juss mek a fuss of 'im fost while I mek us a brew, then ee'll leave us be, while we're sat.' Ned rolled on his back and presented his belly and genitals for inspection.

'It's about that thing that's bin doing all the killing is it?' asked the older man, dispensing with the emollient pleasantries and formalities of conversation in the time-honoured tradition of rural Yorkshiremen. Jackson envied the older man's directness with a mixture of unquestioning admiration and envy.'

'Since I'm not the countryman that you are Jack, I'm thinking of getting an expert in from outside the county. Someone with a fresh pair of eyes.'

'Outsider eh? Why would you be doing a thing like that? You might as well say us folk can't handle our own problems.'

'I know people will say things like that Mr Farrar, but if it's an outsider people can't accuse them of favouritism. And a stranger wouldn't have any history or loyalties that might cause what I like to call invisible grievances, if you know what I mean…'

'Not as daft as ya look, are ya lad?'

'There's another reason Mr Farrar. There's never been anything like this happen, this far north.'

'Some folks, who've read their local 'istory might 'ave something ta say ta thee about that.'

'Well, I'm ready to listen to anyone or anything if it helps us stop these attacks.'

Chapter Twenty-Five

Exmoor

'Chudleigh Farm, Missus Burr speaken…'

'Hello Mrs Burr. It's PC Alger, Jackson Alger. I spoke with you yesterday if you recall… Could I speak to your husband if he's home now?'

'Ees jus' in the boot room cleaning up, Constable. Let me av yorr number thurr, where you're at?'

'It's Whitby 77659.'

'An' what's the code?'

'Oh yes, my apologies– it's 0947.'

'Now– be s'gudd as t'ang up– an' oi'll ring 'eee back, drectly.'

'I can wait Mrs Burr, it's no trouble.'

'No, oid loike eee t'ang up. Then I'll ring eee back, say 'ello– then 'ang up. Then you can ring us back. By toime we've done all thart, John should be spick an'span.'

'I don't understand…'

'We gets a lotta pranksters calling uz Mr Alger – cuz o' what John does, this way we knows ooo we're speaken to, so…'

'So I'll hang up – then you ring me back – hear my voice again, then hang up. Then I ring you?'

'You got 'em. Whenever you loike…'

A few minutes later, Jackson had Mr Burr.

'Mr Burr? Good to speak to you at…'

'The wife sez yoos a constable, frum North Yorkshire Police.'

'That's right Mr Burr. Part of our area covers Kettleness.'

'Kettle – ness… where's that to then?'

'We're a few miles north of Whitby sir.'

'Whitby eh? Cold up thurr I 'spect. Most o' the yerr…'

'Yes it can be quite bracing. *Fresh* certainly…'

'You knows where oi am then, t'other end o' the map. I s'pect yull be wanning ta ask me summen about big cats. We only get one kind o' letter or phone call west o' Taunton. You thinks you got one, 'ave eee?'

'Er, well, that could be one possible explanation. I'd really appreciate your discretion, by the way.'

'These things iz no big deal, down yerr n'more, Mr Alger. Big cats iz a fact o' life an' everyone knows it. 'Cept they arse'oles at the Ministry of Ag, theym pretend loike they don't exist, cos if they did, the buggers would 'ave to do summen' about 'em? Can't say I ever 'eard one so far north as you got though. Mus' be 'ardy bastard – scuze moi English.'

'We're not absolutely certain that we have a big cat yet Mr Burr. That's why I'd like to keep this to ourselves. It might not be a big cat problem at all; there's a strong possibility it could even be a wolf, or even a bear.'

'A bear..? Bugger me – I think you'd know if you 'ad a bear!' Bears is 'uge inem? Don't know too much about bears, cept 'em being omnivores. If yull scuze me for being blunt, you'd ave ta be a proper fool to mistake one with t'other.'

'There have been a few sightings of a large wolf-like

animal recently– in the village of Cloughton. I should add there is a zoo nearby and they do have a wolf pack.'

'Sounds as tho' yoo got yer answer already then done' it. There's not much more I could tell eee.'

'There's just one problem with the wolf theory, it doesn't fit the witness reports. It has been reported by several witnesses as being a wolf of considerable size– *considerable size*. The size of a lion.'

'Size of a lion eh? Safe ta say yoo won't be using Kitekat ta bait the bastard then…'

Jackson respectfully ignored the farmer's joke and ploughed on. 'Do panthers or cougars compare in size to lions, Mr Burr?'

'Well… Alsatians look pretty much like a wolf frum a long ways off, 'specially at dusk. I seen some Alsatians round yerr that'd make you shit yourself. When you says "wolf-like" how's that diff'rent from a wolf – have you made any casts?'

'Casts?'

'Plaster casts. From its tracks. That's one way o'settlin' it.'

'I really wouldn't know what to look for Mr Burr. We don't, well – as yet we haven't had any forensic examinations from the crime scenes. The scenes of the killings aren't really crime scenes as such, just remains. The ground around them wasn't protected of course, so they were all covered in wellington boot prints and tyre tracks by the time I arrived much later. When I say a wolf of considerable size, it's been described by witnesses as being half-bear, half-wolf.'

'Half-bear, half-wolf you say… You got yurr work cut out then? Oi'm a sort of unofficial authority on big cats down yer– so striped elephants an' bear-wolves'ez not sumthen oi've come 'cross,' said Mr Burr guardedly, unsure whether he was being played as a fool.

'Granted,' replied Jackson, refusing to rise to the smoothly delivered jibe from the farmer, whom he was still desperate to keep on side. I just hoped you could tell me something about big cats feeding habits.'

'Well, oi spose oi could spare a foo minutes. Oim guessin' this is free advice oim gevven out – izzit?'

'I've not been authorised to employ any experts yet sir. I'm just hoping people are willing to give of themselves to help.'

'If oi wuz ta 'give of moiself' as you puts it, we'd all be on benefetts Mr Alger.'

'Ahhh, perhaps we could come to an arrangement. I could propose you as an independent expert, and if you were invited to work for us on that basis we would certainly cover your fee and expenses. For a reasonable sum. I could put it to my sergeant, if that's acceptable to *you* of course.'

'Problem is see, we're lambing, so oi can't leave the farm.'

'Oh. Do you mean you could only work over the phone?'

'Look– I'll tell eee as much as I knows this ways. Send us a cast o' the prints if you should foind another, an' I'll look it over. If you needs anyone to find the bastard, I knows a gudd tracker who'd be willing to travel. I don't much like being more than a couple of hours away from 'ome anyways. Away from the family an' the farm. If eee can work round that, then we can get along. Oive written a book on the cats, you'd probably have to order it where you're at. You'll need about ten copies…'

'TEN?'

'Ten's good. I'll be able to give of moiself much better

furr ten. Fifteen or twenty an' you'll find me very 'elpful indeed…'

'How much are they?'

'Fifteen pounds. *The Big Cats of Devon*. Tarka Publishing. Your bookshop can order 'em.'

'Does this tracker friend of yours have any hunting experience?'

'Been hunting since he was a bay– Dubby. Ex-army snoiper too, clever fella.'

'Bay? Sorry, I don't…'

'Youngster.'

'Does he have a firearms licence?'

'Well, you'd 'ope 'umdid, 'im 'avin so many guns an' all. You should see the thing he killed this lynx with, lovely looken rifle. Bullets as big as a Castella. Got to be tooled up for this game. You won't get rid o' buggers like they big cats with a pasty an' a caution.'

'What's his name Mr Burr?'

'Dudley Kingcome, Dubby. Lives just outsoide Torrington. He's a sparky. I can give eee his phone number.'

'A sparky?'

'Aye, 'lectrician…'

'Oh!.. I see! Yes–that might be useful – thank you very much…'

Since he was tall enough to hold a rifle, Dudley Kingcome had shot all manner of things for money. A quiet, self-contained farm boy, from the heart of rural Devon, he had spent all his productive waking hours outdoors. For farmers, he shot injured livestock. For the army, he shot farmers, but only those who were members of the IRA. Since passing through the Army Sniper School, he had sent twenty-eight wellington-shod terrorists and bomb makers into the green fields and lanes of the afterlife – all in the sitting position. The majority in vans or lorries and five in tractors. Dudley was good at his craft, because he was patient, and because he had come from the same stock as his victims. He knew how to use dung to mask his scent from the farm dogs which belonged to his targets and he knew the chores and routines of farm life. He had even used the faeces of one of his victim's own dogs. He was, in his own particular way, a bolt action death dealer – in shit. Dudley's last kill for the army had left a mark on the borderlands of Northern Ireland equal to any scar on the battlegrounds of northern France – for the cost of a single round. Lance Corporal Kingcome and his spotter had tracked two enormous fertiliser bombs and a terrorist hit squad from their hide in a nettle-filled orchard on a hill in County Armagh, and realised they were about to pass each other on opposite sides of the B1277 near Dorsey. After seeking permission to engage, he sent an incendiary bullet through the thin metal skin of the passing car's fuel tank which set off an explosion that threw the remains of the car and the lorries into the adjoining fields and created a crater big enough to close the circuit road beside Black Pig's Dyke for eight months. The pressure wave of the blast was so strong that it peeled back the hedges and turf on the surrounding pasture for a distance of eighty-five feet.

It was one of the most remarkable goodbyes in the history of his trade, yet for all his commendations, his medals and his willingness to keep going back to one of the most dangerous theatres of war, when the time came for Dudley to say goodbye to his life in the army, both he and his superiors breathed a sigh of relief, although his skills were celebrated with pride, the vessel in which they resided had never reflected his Regiment's idea of a regular soldier. Dudley was never deliberately untidy. Rather, he had an untidy physicality– and a posture that could not be altered either by nature, force, or training; or by the showers of obscenities thrown his way by the non-commissioned officers (his immediate superiors) whose clumsy insults and biting sarcasm were so ineffective in correcting his perceived shortcomings. In uniform, he had been as much of a scruff as the army had ever tolerated – a man who could ruin a parade standing still, with his ambling bow-legged slouch and lopsided gait that had made his turning-out parade so entertaining. It was only his skill with a rifle which kept him from civvy street before he reached his ninth year.

Once his discharge had been processed, Dudley returned to Devon and moved back to his parents' dairy farm near Honiton, taking on some of the duties his father was beginning to struggle with, as his father and his father's father had also done. He had not yet provided the family with an heir; an irritation that was always at the back of his mind. But he couldn't yet comprehend the importance of attending the various dances organised by the local farming community's social club, despite his mother's hints and his father's verbal prods, though Dudley, who was wiser than he seemed, decided to bide his time and pick up a divorcee when the time came, someone whose fertility was already proven, and who was less fussy about a man's physical shortcomings, if they came with a profitable farm.

'Phone Dudley! Some Grockle frum Yorkshire. Says eeez with the police.'

'Police Ma?'

'That's what eee sez. What you bin doin'..?'

'What've oi bin doin'?' Looken' after eee. That's what oi bin doin'.'

'You not shot n'body bay?'

'Pack it in Ma…'

'Better speak to 'um then, afore eee rings off. Might be money ennett.'

Dudley tramped into the boot room of his parents' farmhouse and picked up the receiver on the shelf.

"LO?"

'Dudley Kingcome?'

'Ooos thess?'

'My name's Alger, Mr Kingcome. Jackson Alger. I'm with North Yorkshire Police, sir.'

'With 'em eh?'

'I'm the community officer for Staithes, Runswick Bay and Kettleness. A friend of yours, a Mr Burr, gave me your phone number. I believe you've hunted and tracked some non-native species of big cats?

'Moight do…'

'I really could do with your help Mr Kingcome, I think that we could have a big cat problem in my district. I have a proposition for you, if you'd like to hear it? If you'd consider it we'd all be very grateful.'

'Proposition..? Just so's we understands each other Mister Alger, this is a payin' job izzit?'

Chapter Twenty-Six

The Contract

'Hello Jack.'

'Conn.'

'I went to the Church in Whitby.'

'You 'ad enough time ta see it all then? I can tell by the look on ya face – d'you 'ave time to read the other stuff?'

'Aye, I did.'

'Well, now you know,what I know – what are you gonna do about it?'

'I shouldn't think there's anything to be done, d' you Jack?'

'At least thee can protect thi' sen'. Till it stops. Jackson's trying to get a hunter on the case. Some bloke from Devon.'

'Someone ta shoot it?'

'I know what you're gonna say next, but this fella's an ex-army sniper.'

'But…'

'If you were ta put this fella up Conn. On yer land, then we can mek sure he uses the reet kind o' bullet.'

'You mean a silv…'

'Explosive bullet. Tek off the head, tek out the heart. Turn the heart inta ash in yer stove. That's the way it's done.'

It took another week of telephone calls, an exchange of letters and a brown envelope of used notes before Dudley was finally welcomed into the small community of Kettleness and installed in readiness. Dudley decided to use Conn Thatcher's static caravan as his base. It was far enough away from the main farmhouse and outbuildings to put him on the front line in his game of cat and mouse; yet was still connected to all the farm's services and offered the kind of comforts he had never enjoyed before 'in country' on the Irish borderlands. To a hunter like Dudley, its proximity to the stream and its view of the riverbank and flood plain gave him a major advantage; it also meant he could fart as much as he liked and stay warm and comfortable while he was watching the field boundary with his spotter scope, by the biggest window.

Dudley knew that large predatory mammals always hunted close to water sources – within their own ranges – and always preferred to drink, on the inside curve, of the same well-covered riverbanks; away from the pounding noise of white water or waterfalls, but close to woods or undergrowth that offered cover for stalking or concealment. The big cats he had stalked in the wilds of Devon always struck within ten or twenty feet of woodland or thick undergrowth, where their scent could not be spread easily by the wind. And never attacked or approached across open country. In many respects, they were using the same skills as Dudley, but killing for food rather than a commission, or a tepid plate of eggs, chips and beans.

Just as he had done in the Army, Dudley kept the same maintenance and cleaning regimen for his own gun, a bolt-action Remington 700, the rifle beloved of military snipers and deer hunters the world over for its accuracy and robustness.

Sitting down at the table, in Conn Thatcher's static caravan, Dudley unpacked his weapon and opened his fishing tackle box, selecting two felt cleaning plugs which he placed on a clean newspaper, before dousing them in Tri-Flon lubricating oil, pushing one through the barrel with a wooden dowel and repeating the procedure with the second plug. Dudley also checked, cleaned and lubricated the breech and bolt mechanisms until he was satisfied with the operation of the bolt and the ejector. Next, he fitted an arrester block behind the rear telescopic scope mount, which was designed to stop 'scope creep' then cleaned and loaded the magazine, inspected his ammunition and chambered a round. Once the rifle was ready, he applied the safety catch and home-made guard which kept branches and twigs away from his trigger. Dudley preferred a very short amount of travel, with a 2lb pull. Finally, he attached the sling, bound the barrel and stock in scraps of camouflage cloth, covered his scope with a black 40-denier stocking, to stop moonlight reflecting off the lens of the telescopic sight, then waited for sundown.

Fifteen miles away, in the great study of Charlwood House, Lord William Henry Warner Woollens pulled the brake on the library ladder rail, and ascended the steps to the fourth collection, second tier bookcases, which housed the family's literature and records collection, covering the reigns of Henry VIII and Elizabeth I.

Lord Warner Woollens put on his reading spectacles and scanned the six shelves of the fourth-placed bookcase, selecting a torso-sized volume titled *England, Scotland and*

Spain, in War and Peace, 1500-1700 for the lift basket, then he placed a 5lb ingot on the hook of the counterweight rope, pulled out the anchor peg on the book lift and let the basket glide down to the floor.

Once at his desk, he unlocked the clasp on the cover and began to read. After two hours and half a bottle of Auslese, he put the book aside, and from his desk drawer pulled on a pair of disposable gloves, of the type used by scholars to study priceless manuscripts and fragile documents. Then the study door swung back and his wife floated into the room in a great knot of fabric and brocade.

'Gloves, William? I sincerely hope you're not about to play doctors and nurses again. It's rather late to be inserting your hands in the animals– is it not?'

'I am wearing gloves for the purpose of examining an artefact, from the estate. Be so kind as to close the door on your way out Antonia.'

'I've no interest in artefacts William. I was just curious to discover where *you* were.'

'I'm here…Goodnight.'

Once he was alone again, Lord Woollens tipped the gold doublon from a small tupperware box onto a sheet of vellum, placed a sheet of rubbing paper over the coin and dragged a stick of fine charcoal backwards and forwards over the paper covering the coin, to obtain an image. Satisfied with his work, he replaced the coin in the tupperware container and locked it in his desk.

'The Treasure of the Mar del Norte…' he whispered, 'it can't be. It had better not b-be.' Then he put the rubbing in the top drawer of his desk and turned off the lamp.

'Buggeryomlettes…'

In the empty void below the DJ's island inside Mystery City, the evil root of the hidden gold began to disseminate its malignant oeuvre, splitting the insulation on the electrical wiring beneath the turntables, while it pumped out a sluggish, dewy fog through the seams of the toolbox in which it was trapped. A half bottle of Napoleon brandy toppled over and began to pool onto the chipboard base of the vented bargeboard, then the first sparks began to fall.

Barnett woke up suddenly in his bed, and propped himself up on his elbows. Ears pricked. Only the snores of his PVA-smeared chum James Stone disturbed the silence. But Barnett sensed danger and swung his legs out of bed. Pulling on his Celtic football dressing gown. He grasped the machete he always kept under his pillow and stood up, sniffing the air.

Bibliography

Ackroyd, Peter, *'Civil War: The History of England Volume III.'* Pan Books, 2015.

Fenton, Sasha, *'Moon Signs.'* The Aquarian Press, 1987.

Wheatley, Dennis, *'The Devil Rides Out.'* Bloomsbury Publishing PLC, 2013.

Fortune, Dion, *'Glastonbury: Avalon of the Heart.'* The Aquarian Press, 1989.

Carley, James, *'Glastonbury Abbey: The Holy House at the Head of the Moors Adventurous.'* Guild Publishing, 1988.

Watson, Lyall, *'Supernature, a Natural History of the Supernatural.'* Hodder and Stoughton, 1973.

Sargent, Carl, *'The Astrology of Rising Signs.'* Century Hutchinson Ltd, 1986.

Murray, Williamson, *'The Luftwaffe, Strategy for Defeat, 1933 -1945,'* Eagle editions Ltd, 2003.

Rimington, Stella. *'Open Secret: The Autobiography of the Former Director General of MI5.'* London: Hutchinson, 2001.

Le Carre, John, *'Tinker, Tailor, Soldier, Spy.'* Sceptre, 2011.

Columbo, Franco. *'The Bodybuilder's Nutrition Book.'* Contemporary Books Inc, 1985.

Dewar, Michael, Lt Col RGI. *'The British Army in Northern Ireland,'* Arms and Armour Press, 1985.

The Order of Bards, Ovates and Druids.

Whitborough on Sea Principal Street Index

West Court
Westgate
Whapple Bank
Whelping Way
Whispering Gate
Wicked Tree
Wilson Terrace
Wray Terrace

Z
Zeppelin Row